D1485162

PHILIP WYLIE:
Pearls

Dishonor among thieves foils an ingeniously planned robbery in this hilarious story about crime among the upper classes.

LLEWELLYN HUGHES:
Released from
Chancery

A chilling tale of the supernatural, with a very different kind of ghost.

BUDD SCHULBERG:
Spotlight

A touching portrait of an old film idol, and his unexpected moment of glory.

Preachers, card sharks, home-town girls, flying aces, floozies, U.S. marshals and Mom: name a character and you'll find his story in this fabulous collection by the top writers of the twenties and thirties. Full of native American wit and earthy humor, written in the tradition of Mark Twain and O. Henry, they provide a dynamic picture of life in the United States in the days before World War II.

Outstanding Short Stories in
SIGNET Editions

SELECTED STORIES OF JEAN STAFFORD

Sixteen stories, ranging from Colorado to Germany,
from the world of the child to that of the adult, by a
writer hailed by critics as one of the best in America.
(#T2830—75¢)

BUBBLE GUM AND KIPLING *by Tom Mayer*

Stories about a young man of the American Southwest,
some of which have appeared in *Harper's, The New
Yorker,* and *Story Magazine.* (#P2769—60¢)

THE INJUSTICE COLLECTORS (The Unholy Three)
by Louis Auchincloss

Eight superb short stories about men and women sub-
consciously drawn to self-punishment. By the author
of *The Rector of Justin.* (#P2676—60¢)

SHORT FRIDAY AND OTHER STORIES
by Isaac Bashevis Singer

Remarkable tales, translated from the Yiddish, in
which demons, witches and angels turn up in everyday
life, whether it is lived in a Polish village or in Brooklyn. (#T2770—75¢)

TO OUR READERS: If your dealer does not have the
SIGNET and MENTOR books you want, you may order
them by mail enclosing the list price plus 10¢ a copy to
cover mailing. (New York City residents add 5% Sales
Tax. Other New York State residents add 2% plus any
local sales or use taxes.) If you would like our free cat-
alog, please request it by postcard. The New American
Library, Inc., P. O. Box 2310, Grand Central Station,
New York, N. Y. 10017.

FAMOUS SHORT SHORT STORIES

Compiled by

FRANK C. PLATT

A SIGNET BOOK

Published by The New American Library,
New York and Toronto
The New English Library Limited, London

Copyright 1929, 1931, Liberty Weekly, Inc.

Copyright 1931, 1932, 1933, 1934, 1935, Liberty Publishing
Corporation

Copyright 1936, 1937, 1938, 1939, 1940, 1941, 1942,
MacFadden Publications, Inc.

Copyright 1943, 1944, 1945, 1946, 1947, 1948, 1949, 1950,
Liberty Magazine, Inc.

Copyrights renewed by Liberty Library Corporation

Copyright © 1966 Liberty Library Corporation. All rights
reserved. No part of this book may be reproduced in any
form without written permission.

First Printing, April, 1966

SIGNET TRADEMARK REG. U.S. PAT. OFF. AND FOREIGN COUNTRIES
REGISTERED TRADEMARK—MARCA REGISTRADA
HECHO EN CHICAGO, U.S.A.

SIGNET BOOKS are published *in the United States* by
The New American Library, Inc.,
1301 Avenue of the Americas, New York, New York 10019,
in Canada by The New American Library of Canada Limited,
295 King Street East, Toronto 2, Ontario,
in the United Kingdom by The New English Library Limited,
Barnard's Inn, Holborn, London, E. C. 1, England

PRINTED IN THE UNITED STATES OF AMERICA

CONTENTS

PEARLS

Philip Wylie

CEDRIC BRADLEY, at fifty-three, was short and bowlegged, apple-cheeked, with bland blue eyes and a cockney accent occasionally audible in his staccato speech. He controlled Bradley, Ltd., the largest and most magnificent jewelry house in London. He had two boasts: his own hand and brain had built the business; and in all the romantic progress of the affair he had never been swindled or robbed.

On a certain morning in May, when Piccadilly poets were thinking of the lilacs at Kew and Bradley was estimating the profits in carved lapis lazuli, the card of Lord Throckmorton of Taine was presented to the jeweler. Throckmorton was ushered in—a tall, tan, rectilinear man with a monocle engraved in his right eye. He was a total stranger to the firm.

Mr. Bradley and Lord Throckmorton moved leisurely through the commonplaces to business.

"Bradley—I say—my daughter is about to be married."

"Your daughter. Of course."

"Beautiful thing, Gwen is. Shameful life I've led her. We've been twenty years in Australia. Just brought her to London a fortnight ago. First time in her life. And now I've got to pop off to Africa for three months. Must make amends, eh? Giving you carte blanche to help me out, Bradley. A necklace, I thought. Pearls, what? Matched and perfect. Nothing unusual—just the best."

Mr. Bradley's bland eyes became more lifeless and opaque. He said, "Quite."

Throckmorton of Taine stared at the ceiling. "I thought—with three months—you could—er—assemble something decent. About—er—say eighty thousand pounds—what?"

Mr. Bradley's fingers lifted and fell. "Quite," he repeated.

His Lordship extracted a checkbook from his coat. "A deposit, what?" He did not seem to perceive the answering nod. "Say—ten thousand?" Another nod. The check was written. The two men shook hands. A liveried doorman presently ushered the angular Australian into his town car.

Three months passed. Lord Throckmorton entered the establishment of Bradley, Ltd., with a vacant air that vanished only momentarily when the head of the firm exhibited the necklace. "Good Lord, Bradley, they're rather fine!"

"The best."

"I say—my wife's an invalid. Wanted her to see them before Gwen. Perhaps you could send them over?"

Bradley gazed at the finest string of matched pearls he had ever made. "I'd be glad to bring them over myself."

Throckmorton smiled. "Splendid. Tea, or something. I'll ask her Ladyship."

The little jeweler received a note from Lady Throckmorton, and was received by Lord Throckmorton in the drawing-room. Her Ladyship was wheeled in; a winsome vivacious cripple. She wept when she saw the pearls. A nurse took her away presently and Bradley pocketed the pearls. Lord Throckmorton asked to see them again and was rhapsodizing when his daughter called, "Oh, father!"

A minute alarm crossed his face. The pearls were to be a surprise at the time of the wedding. Hastily his Lordship dropped them into the drawer of a cabinet that had belonged to Louis XV. Both he and his guest rose to meet the Right Honorable Gwendolyn. She was more than an elegant girl; she was gorgeous. Bradley was exalted, an emotion that gave him the look of placid contentment. The butler served tea and later Throckmorton asked his daughter to sing.

Her father sat near the piano. "Play that old thing I like," he suggested. The butler tiptoed to his side and whispered. Throckmorton nodded, lifted his hands in pantomime apology, and slipped out of the room. Gwen sang on.

It was a long rendition and Bradley listened with his eyes half closed. Gwen finished, glanced at her single auditor, and began another song. When she was half finished, she stopped. "Where's father?"

"He was called out."

"How ridiculous! Excuse me—I'll bring him right back." She left the chamber.

Five minutes passed and then ten. A hollow quiet slowly permeated the house. Bradley paced the floor. By and by he pulled the bell cord. No response. A thought struck him. He went to the Louis XV cabinet and pulled the drawer open. The pearls were gone!

It was not a drawer, in fact, but a sort of chute, lined with silk so that the pearls would not rattle as they slid into the adjacent room. Mr. Bradley walked out to the hall and picked up his hat and stick. Twilight was descending upon

London as he opened the carved door that bore the bogus arms of Throckmorton of Taine.

He hailed a cab. At his own apartment the butler swung the door wide and Bradley went somewhat petulantly to his bedroom. He pushed a picture aside, opened the safe behind it, took the bona fide string of matched pearls from his coat pocket, and locked them behind the steel door. When the picture had been replaced he mopped his brow with a silk handkerchief. Then he allowed himself the relaxation of a good, round oath in which cockney predominated.

CHECKMATE

Samuel W. Taylor

THE throbbing of his left great toe brought the deputy marshal awake. He speculated dimly whether this bunk, these blankets, the cabin roof beams above him, the sizzle and smell of frying bacon were all parts of a delicious hallucination. But were he still out in the strong cold, that toe would not throb. It had been the first part of him to signal the treachery of false warmth as he stumbled along in the arctic snow.

He rolled his head and saw the big man fussing with the skillet at the sheet-iron stove. The big man had matted red hair and a curly beard. He was Trench Roberts. The deputy had been brought out of the cold by the man for whom he was searching.

The big man turned from the stove, grinned through his curly red beard. "That was close," he said. "Lucky my dogs picked up your scent as I turned into the gulch. I'll bet you could eat. Say, do you play chess?"

Days passed. When the deputy's left great toe began going green, the big man did a bit of neat surgery with a hammer and chisel. The big man taught him chess, and through the long nights the deputy would sit staring at the board, absently cracking his knuckles, trying to think of chess and not the other problem.

The big man had hung the deputy's revolver and holster on a wall peg by the bunk. Once, when the big man was out, the deputy ascertained the weapon was loaded.

A month went by. The deputy knew he could travel. He became moody.

"You can't play chess worth sawdust," the big man grinned one night. "Watch out for your queen."

"Look here, Trench!" the deputy exploded. "No use beating around the bush. You know I am after you. This is working on me. I've got to take you in, Trench."

"Sure—duty and all that." The big man kept grinning. "Go ahead; it's your move."

"Look here, Trench. Why did you kill that partner of yours?" The deputy was groping for an out. "It wasn't just cold-blooded murder like they say it was?"

The big man shrugged. "Old Bill was a nice guy, too, but he drove me wild. I taught him chess that winter we stayed together, and by Christmas we were nip and tuck. I remember one game . . ."

"Never mind about that. Why did you kill him?"

"Why, he wouldn't wash his socks. Two men in a cabin all winter, and he wouldn't wash his socks. Finally it was too much. It drove me wild."

The deputy cracked his knuckles, pondering.

"Did you kill Loftus, the other deputy who went after you last year?"

"It was either him or me."

"Why the hell did you bring me in out of the snow?" the deputy growled.

"I wouldn't just leave a man to die, would I?" Then the big man flashed his grin. "Anyhow, I'm a friendly cuss. Looked like I'd found a chess partner."

The deputy got up from the table, turned to the wall and drew his revolver from the holster hanging by the peg. He gave the big man plenty of chance to get the rifle in the far corner of the cabin. But when he turned the big man hadn't moved.

"You're under arrest, Trench Roberts," the deputy muttered. He felt a bit foolish, but he went on doggedly: "I'm taking you to Fairbanks to stand trial for murder."

"You'll feel better after dinner," the big man soothed. "Come on. Let's finish this game."

"I mean it. I've got to take you in, regardless."

"Why?"—blandly curious.

"You're a nice guy and I really like you. I owe you my life. But you've still murdered two men and I'm a deputy United States marshal. I just never learned how to cheat myself."

"Upward and onward," the big man said.

The deputy wet dry lips. "Tagging it don't help. I can't cheat, one way or the other. If I don't take you back, then I just won't go back myself."

"Fine!" beamed the big man. "Fine! You stay here with me, and we'll play a lot of chess."

The deputy hadn't meant it that way. "I've got things to go back to. A job. Friends. Something they call self-respect. And—well, there's a wife and baby."

"Poof!" The big man spread his hands. "I've left two wives, three kids! Shucks, you forget 'em. Come on. Let's finish this game. And watch your queen. Or," the big man added softly, "shoot me now and get it over with. Let's settle this foolishness."

They played a lot of chess during the winter. The deputy viciously disciplined his mind in that one channel. After the New Year he never lost a game. The big man became morose and sullen. For almost a month in the early spring he communicated only in grunts and gestures.

Then one day the deputy was hunched over the board, cracking his knuckles while he studied his play, when the big man arose, went around the table. The deputy glanced up just as the big man rushed with the upraised ax.

"Quit popping them knuckles!" he screamed, bringing the ax down.

Jerking back, the deputy felt the blade brush his hair before sinking deeply into the thick table top. The ax stuck in the plank just long enough for the deputy to come around and up, slugging. That was long enough.

He handcuffed the crumpled figure of the big man.

"All right, pal," the deputy said grimly. "Now I can take you in. Now we're quits."

SPOTLIGHT

Budd Schulberg

THE director was trying to bring the picture through in twenty-nine days. The assistant director was trying to impress the director. The second assistant was trying to prove his right to be a first assistant. The three hundred extras were trying to please everybody. The ten-dollar people were trying to fight their way into focus. The seven-and-a-halfs were walking briskly back and forth, doing their perspiring best.

"All right, folks, get *moving!*" the second assistant

screamed. "Now watch me. When I wave this handkerchief, start walking as if you expected to get somewhere."

"What're ya watching him for?" the first assistant yelled. "When *I* drop my hand, start talking it up. You're all happy, see? And make it good! We gotta finish by six sharp."

The director, running sweat, sleeves rolled up, paced impatiently. "What's the trouble, boys?" he barked. "I'm half a day behind now. Get the lead out."

It was another of those scorching Hollywood afternoons. One of those tough, irritable days. The extras had been at it since nine that morning. When the long-awaited recess came, they crowded around the water cooler.

"After you," a florid-faced, white-haired old man offered politely. When he was almost trampled in the rush, he took his place philosophically at the end of the line. He mopped his face professionally with an edge of his handkerchief. His calm silence was like a wall of glass cutting him off from the whirlpool of excitement all around him.

Even at the call, "Take your places, everybody," he displayed not the slightest trace of emotion. He straightened the dress suit he wore and took his place in the line again.

When the director said, "Pick me out some people for flash reactions," excitement stirred the crowd. For some it might mean the chance they had waited and struggled for. For others it meant the extra fifteen dollars they would earn if they were asked to speak a line.

As the old man saw the assistant director descending on him, he waited docilely, like an old horse about to be saddled. But he wasn't sure he wanted this unexpected momentary spotlight. He was old and tired, and this meant strong lights in his eyes and the strain of having to learn new words and speak them within the next few minutes.

But even as he hoped the assistant wasn't going to single him out for a close-up, he was praying that he would. Because extra work had become scarcer and scarcer through the summer; his last job had been two ten-dollar days three weeks ago. That meant pressing the dress suit yourself, and stalling the landlady. Now this additional fifteen dollars would be the difference between keeping the room and packing up again.

Then the assistant was on him. "All right, Pop, we'll use you." He stepped into the glare, waiting quietly with eyes half closed as the director opened up on him.

"Okay, old-timer. This'll all be over in a minute—we hope.

All you've got to do is smile and say, 'I've been waiting here thirty years for this,' and he gives you the cue, 'On this very spot?' and then you give it this—watch me." And the director turned his head toward the floor and then quickly looked up again with an unexpected change of expression. "Get it? Just a different version of that old double take."

The old man nodded his head slowly. He said he thought he got it.

"Then let's go. See if we can't get it in the can the first time," the director said, as the juicers hit the lights. He crouched below the cameras, watching the old man critically.

"Hold it. Cut!" he yelled. "You forgot that double take. Try it again."

More nervously, the old man tried again. "I've been thirty years——"

"For Pete's sake! You forgot *'waiting'!* Waiting—what you're making us do! Take it once more."

The old man nodded, wetting his lips, trembling. He began again. And again. The director fumed internally. Typical studio economy! Trying to save money with a ten-buck extra instead of paying an actor to do it! The old man fumbled the scene worse each time. He was trying too hard.

"Look, pal. You're making it too tough for yourself. It's just one quick take, see? Just that famous old trick with your eyes and a turn of your head. The thing what's-his-name, Willie Robbins, originated in the old silent days. Think you can do it?"

"I—I think I can do it now," the old man said.

Everybody hushed again. The cameras started rolling. He made one more tentative stab at it. In vain.

"All right!" the director roared. "Get back in the crowd —we'll try somebody else."

And as the old man tried to disappear inconspicuously, he heard the director say, "For heaven's sake get someone who knows what a double take is!" And an eager, confident extra took his place in the scene.

Back in the crowd of extras, he stood watching his successor. Just in front of him a dumpy elderly woman, one of the visitors to the set, was approaching the handsome young star with her autograph book opened. In a kind of reflex action, the star smiled and reached out for the book. But she had already gone by him! The old man looked up at her in surprise.

"I never thought I'd actually meet you—after all these years," she said, and she held up the book.

For a moment he stared at her unbelievingly, and then, as he took the book and began to write in it, he seemed to grow broader and taller. He wrote silently, "As ever, Willie Robbins," handed the book back with a faint smile, and turned to watch the successful completion of the scene.

ME AND NINE HUNDRED DOLLARS

Oscar Schisgall

I WOKE up in a ditch about two miles from Longhorn City, and the sorrel cayuse was nibbling grass a few feet away, and I felt awful. My sombrero and six-gun had slipped to the bottom of a hollow, but I was too dizzy to go after them.

Then I remembered my money belt.

I pretty near collapsed in pure fright. Because the money was gone! My uncle's money, which I was supposed to deliver to Ned Gordon of the Bar G Bar, was gone!

I looked around like a wild man. Hunting in the ditch and underbrush did no good. And then, all of a sudden, I remembered the two strangers—two lanky hombres who'd been drinking with me in the Lucky Horse Saloon. Last thing I could recollect was going out of the place with them; they were holding my arms, because I was wobbly as a scarecrow after putting down all that liquor. And I had a hazy idea that the three of us had ridden out of Longhorn City together, singing to the Arizona stars.

I gathered up my gun and sombrero right quick, swung into the saddle, and hightailed into Longhorn City with a kind of fever in my head. When I rushed into the saloon, there was Baldy behind the bar, calm as usual.

"Baldy," I yelled, all hoarse, "you remember the two polecats I was drinkin' with last night?"

Baldy quit wiping the bar. "Sure, Slim," he said. "Why? Did they rob you too?"

"Too?" I said. "What d'you mean, too?"

"Four o'clock this mornin'," said Baldy, "they busted into the bank. Got quite a bit o' cash. Got away. Nobody knows where. Sheriff Dunn's out huntin' with a posse."

I leaned against the bar and held my head and groaned. Baldy slid a drink under my nose.

"On the house," he said. "How much did they take for?"

"Nine hundred dollars! My uncle," I sort of moaned, "bought some beef from Ned Gordon. He was payin' for it in cash. He couldn't go himself yesterday, so he sent me to Gordon's. But my horse went lame on the way, an' I had to walk eleven miles to borrow another at the Circle T, so it was 'most midnight when I got to town. I figured I wouldn't wake Ned Gordon up so late. Figured I'd wait till mornin' to pay him."

"An' meanwhile," said Baldy, "you drifted in here an' had a few drinks with them strangers." He clucked kind of sadlike and shook his head.

What I'd tell my uncle I didn't know. After the way he'd trusted me, I felt meaner than a tarantula. I went and sat down on the saloon's step, holding my head again.

And then something streaked through my brain like sizzling lightning. I remembered that just before I got real drunk I'd drifted over to a poker table to watch a big hand; and when I got back to the bar, one of the strangers was whispering to the other, "It can't be more'n sixty miles to Phoenix!"

They quit talking when I put my arms around their shoulders.

A minute later I galloped out of Longhorn City and hit the trail for Phoenix.

All morning I pounded the hoofs off the sorrel. By noon the cayuse was about fit to keel over. But I met up with old Mike Stafford, who was riding herd on the Double B spread. He had a fresh horse under him—a fine big bay—and when I explained I was chasing bank robbers he swapped with me pronto.

Two hours later I spotted the strangers.

Yes, sir, caught up with the polecats in a canyon. Their ponies were plumb tuckered out, so that they were traveling slow. They turned quick when they heard me. Reckon they recognized me right off and were plenty scared, because I could hear them curse. They scrambled out of their saddles and pulled iron. I'd won plenty of prize money for shooting down tomato cans at the San Marese rodeo, and I figured at fifty yards I could handle these two. Besides, I was too mad to care. I pulled the bay to a stop and hauled out my six-gun and yelled, "You buzzards give up? Or do I have to come a-blazin'?"

"You come any closer," one of them roared, "an' you'll step into a shower o' lead!"

With that he sent a slug at me by way of warning, and it clicked on a rock. The other hombre started shooting too, but I could see they were firing wild at fifty yards—though one of them did nick my left forearm with a lucky shot. Me, I aimed careful. And after I'd squeezed the trigger four times, both hombres lay squirming.

I walked ahead then and roped them with the riata Mike Stafford had left on the bay's saddle horn. I searched them then and, sure enough, I found the stolen money. Four thousand eight hundred dollars. Nine hundred of it, I figured, was mine, and the rest must belong to the bank. So I put my share in my money belt, buttoned the bank's cash inside my shirt, and headed home, with my prisoners slung over their saddles.

It was past midnight when I got into Longhorn City and turned the two buzzards over to Sheriff Dunn. He was sure surprised. And old man Hornung of the bank swore he'd see I got a suitable reward, and everybody at the Lucky Horse wanted to buy me a drink.

But I said, "Not now, boys, not now. Got to see Ned Gordon at the Bar G Bar first."

So I gave the sheriff the bank's money and rode on alone. Ned was still up. He looked at me with considerable surprise, seeing as how I was dusty and tired and my sleeve was bloodstained.

"Here," I said. "My uncle sent it for that beef."

Ned looked at the money, his eyes popping, then looked at me again. "Doggone it," he said, "you mean to tell me you was so drunk last night you don't remember?"

I said, "Remember what?"

"Why, man, along about two you came over here, woke me out o' sleep, an' put nine hundred dollars into my hands! An' you was so crazy drunk, you rode away singin', without waitin' for so much as a receipt or a thank you!"

THE DANCING MOUSE

Howell N. White, Jr.

PRITCHARD awoke lying fully dressed on a cot in the back room of the Main Street Tavern. He heard voices and laughter from the bar.

He pulled out his watch and focused his bleary eyes. Eleven o'clock. They must have found Paul Manning by now.

Pritchard had not expected Manning's stubborn strength when word arrived that the auditors were coming.

"I won't do it, I tell you, Pritchard!" he had shouted. "I helped you cheat my people, but I'm not going to run away."

"Look here, old man," Pritchard had said. "There's no need of our both getting into trouble. Now, what you need is a drink, eh? Things aren't as black as they look."

And so, last night, Pritchard and Manning had come to the Main Street Tavern. Manning's love of liquor had made it easy for Pritchard to get him drunk, seeming to match drink for drink. Pritchard had pretended drunkenness when he took Manning home, but he had been cold sober when he suggested that Manning needed a ride to clear his head. Manning had been so drunk that he had fallen into a stupor even before Pritchard started the motor, and had not even stirred when Pritchard left, closing the garage doors behind him. Then Pritchard had weaved back to the Main Street Tavern to make good his pretense of drunkenness.

Another burst of laughter came from the bar. Unsteadily Pritchard made his way to the group of men watching something on the polished surface. It was a small dun-colored mouse. Its feet were moving in an odd rhythm.

The eye of Pop Forst, the bartender, lit on Pritchard. "Hello," he said. "You put away enough Scotch last night for two ordinary men. How do you feel?"

Pritchard put a hand to his head. "What you got there?"

"Why, that," said Pop Forst, "is a dancing mouse. Found it jigging around this morning when I came in to clean up. Want a pick-me-up?"

"Lord knows I need one."

When the cop came in, Pritchard did not look up from his drink. The cop's voice was gruff, businesslike:

"You Pritchard?"

The men at the bar stopped talking, forgot the dancing mouse. Pop Forst stopped wiping a glass.

The cop went on: "You're vice president of the water company, aren't you?"

"Yes."

"We've been looking for you. Heard you were with Manning last night. Wanted to tell you he's dead."

Pritchard let his mouth drop open in astonishment.

"A neighbor found him in his garage this morning. Carbon monoxide."

"Good Lord!" said Pritchard with emphasis. "How—why?"

"That's what we want to know. We found out something, though. He was bookkeeper for your company, wasn't he?"

Pritchard nodded.

"The auditors came this morning. They found that the books were screwy. They don't know what the shortage will be; but they know it'll be more than fifty thousand."

Pritchard gasped. "You don't—you can't believe it's suicide!"

"That's what it looked like," said the cop grimly.

"But he couldn't—you—you can't believe——"

"That's right, brother. We don't believe it *was* suicide."

Pritchard clenched his hand on the edge of the bar and held tight. The back of his neck crawled. With an effort he straightened up.

"No," the cop went on, his voice magnified by the background of utter silence, "it wasn't suicide. We found a piece of gravel jammed under the garage door from the outside. Manning couldn't have done that." He paused. "You went home with him, didn't you?"

Pritchard forced a sheepish smile. "Now, officer, I couldn't say. I don't remember."

The cop's face was relentless. "You were seen going home with Manning. Don't say you can't remember."

"Well, officer, I'm ashamed to admit it, but I was drunk. Manning and I both drank too much last night. I may very well have gone home with him as you say, but I don't remember a thing about it. Ask Pop Forst—when I passed out he put me to bed in the back room."

He turned toward the bar for corroboration. The dancing mouse was performing drunkenly, but Pop Forst was not behind the bar.

Pritchard saw him, then, bending down, doing something in the corner where Pritchard had sat last night with Manning. "There's Pop Forst. Ask him whether I was drunk or not."

Only then did Pritchard see what Pop Forst was doing. He had moved the table out from the wall and was tearing up a plank with a pry bar.

"What about it?" said the cop. "Was this guy Pritchard as drunk as he says he was?"

Pop Forst spoke without looking up. "He was drunk all

right. He passed out and I put him to bed in the back room like he says. But"—and a board squealed protestingly as Pop Forst wrenched it up—"he was dead sober until he came back after taking Manning home."

Pritchard shouted desperately, "That's a lie and you know it, you old fool!" What was Pop Forst doing? How could anything have gone wrong?

STILL Pop did not look up. He reached his arm down in the hole he had made in the floor and felt around for something. "I wasn't sure till I found the dancing mouse coming out of a hole over here. Last night Pritchard seemed to be putting away as much Scotch as Manning did rye, but he didn't get drunk. I thought he was faking. This morning I found the proof."

Pritchard was too smart to be bluffed. "Where's your proof, you son——"

Pop Forst straightened up. He thrust a wad of dirty cotton and matted hair under the cop's nose. "The mouse is drunk. Know the smell of Scotch?"

The cop nodded.

"That's what Pritchard was pouring down the mousehole. Take a good smell of the nest, Pritchard."

Pritchard whirled wildly around. There was no escape. The mouse was still dancing. He seized it, hurled it to the floor. Its legs twitched. On its nose there formed, then broke, a drop of blood.

HOMESTRETCH

Lyle Robertson

DANNY REID lay very still, listening to the bugle. The sound of it had guided him back to consciousness. The same urgent strains, repeated over and over—*"Row Guardsman's Mounting,"* the call of the track, bugled summons to sleek mounts to edge into position at the starting gate. He warmed as the tingling notes pumped new strength into his body. He must hoard this strength. He would need it.

The doctor tipped the shade of the hotel room's shabby bridge lamp to throw a cone of light on Danny's face. It was a good face, small, knot-muscled, lined with years, and leathered by so many suns that even its present waxy grayness was tinged with copper. "Fifty-two, eh?" The doctor's skepticism was plain to the hotel manager standing on the other side of Danny's bed.

The manager shrugged. "He's been fifty-two years old— and willing to fight about it—ever since he began stopping here. That was six years ago. Your guess is as good as anybody's. How are chances for him?"

It was the doctor's turn to shrug.

Danny could have answered the question, but he was saving his strength. They wouldn't understand, anyway. It would be like trying to make them hear the bugle, make them understand it. He knew his handicap and he knew ahead of time the outcome of the next race. It was fixed and he could do nothing about it. So he just lay still, listening to the bugle. Then he opened his eyes.

The hotel manager smiled down at him. "Anything you want, Danny?"

"My boots," said Danny. His voice was soft, with just a trace of a rasp. "I want my boots."

The manager looked briefly into the doctor's eyes, then went to the room's cramped clothes closet and came back with Danny's boots. Small and trim they were, like Danny himself. Worn, too. But polished. Black and gleaming. Jockey boots. One of Danny's unsteady hands reached out, took them, hugged them to his chest.

"Thanks," he said. "That's all." He repeated it. The doctor and the manager left the room. The door closed softly after them.

It was hard, getting up and dressing, but Danny did it. Shaking, he tucked stained blue jeans into his shining boots and pulled an old faded suede jacket over a denim shirt. Then, one hand feeling ahead of him against the wall, he made for the door, wishing that he had silks to go with his boots.

In the stairwell he almost fell, but the bugle sustained him. He had heard that bugle, it seemed, as long as he had been able to hear anything. It had called to him as a boy and lured him from home. Countless buglers on countless tracks the country over had filled his ears with it since. It had kindled his blood during the full years when his hard 120 pounds was listed on almost every card. It had stirred him to tears afterward, when nobody remembered him, when he had been willing to do anything, any kind of work, just to keep alive and make the seasonal swing of race meetings. But never had he heard it like this. And he knew why.

"The track." He stumbled as he clambered heavily into the lone taxi.

The driver grinned uncertainly and glanced around to reassure himself that it was nighttime. "There ain't no such thing—this year."

"The track," Danny repeated, and tossed three dollar bills into the front seat. It was the last of his roll. The driver shrugged. The taxi turned into the boulevard and headed east.

The night was one of those chamber of commerce nights —misty, moon-bathed, and still. At the track, soft shadows haunted long rows of low stables. Through them Danny shuffled to the stall of Furbelow, the great three-year-old. The horse nickered as he slipped a light bridle over the tossing head, then stood quietly as his hands caressed the satiny muscled arch of neck. There was no other sound. War having prevented the opening of the meeting, the acres of stables were deserted except for a comparatively few mounts and men.

Silently, haltingly, Danny led the big mare outside and with the help of a bucket got a leg up and mounted. The effort brought a roaring into his head that was all mixed up with the bugle. Through it, vaguely, he realized that Furbelow was saddleless and for a moment or two he was again a youngster galloping bareback on a fat-bellied farm horse. Then, leaning heavily for support, on Furbelow's withers, he urged her toward the track.

A great glass wall of the clubhouse was a sheet of silver in the moonlight ahead of him as he nudged her into position where the starting gate would be. Behind him the mountains were a moon-splashed backdrop. Just before he spanked the mare into her start he saw the needle of a flashlight bobbing toward him from the direction of the stables. That was good. Furbelow would not be allowed to chill—later.

Then Danny ran his race. Unpaced and unstimulated by competition, Furbelow lazed through it, merely exercising. But to Danny she was fire and quicksilver and hurricane. For Danny felt a crowd in the stands, heard the inarticulate roar of its voice. He rode her smart, did Danny, holding her in past the quarter pole, through the backstretch, into the turn. And as the finish line beckoned ahead his voice rose aloud and tear-choked over the singing bugle in his ears, urging her on, sharing his soul with her. She caught his fever and responded, pounding down the stretch in a drumming crescendo. That was how they crossed the line, the big mare fierce and frightening in her speed and Danny crouched low astride her, his heart on fire and tears streaming down his face.

Next day's newspapers covered Danny's race in three sentences:

Furbelow, odds-on favorite to win the now-canceled Santa Bonita Handicap and scheduled to be shipped to an Eastern track later this week, got an unexpected workout late last night when Danny Reid, one-time jockey, spirited her from her stall and took an unexplained gallop around the track. Reid, for many years a track hanger-on, dropped from her back dead of heart failure at the conclusion of the gallop. His meager claim to fame in recent years was his vociferous boast to anyone who would listen that he "had one good race left in him."

THE ROAD TO VALLEY FORGE

Peggy Von Der Goltz

LINNET woke, lay peering into the dark, listening. It's the wind, she told herself—the wind beating that old elm against the house. But she knew it wasn't the wind. Wind didn't sound like marching men. Only British soldiers tramped heavy as the old elm beaten by the wind.

Linnet sat up. British soldiers! Yesterday at sundown Anthony Wayne and a handful of Continentals had passed by, driving cattle up from Jersey to feed the starving men at Valley Forge. Now British soldiers tramped the road behind them. Well-shod, free-moving, the British would catch Mad Anthony by noontime. Linnet jerked on her shoes, wrapped a shawl about her, took the rifle down from its place above the door, loaded it, and rammed home the charge.

"I'll shoot as many redcoats as I can afore they shoot me," she muttered.

Then, suddenly, she dropped the ramrod, stood leaning on the rifle while fury drained out of her, leaving only the dregs of anger. She couldn't go out and fight the British, leaving Johnny and little David to freeze and starve when she was killed. "I must welcome the King's soldiers," she thought, "let them pass on and take Mad Anthony's cattle —seize Valley Forge perhaps."

It was, she reflected, a bitter thing that her man should fight and freeze and starve to gain freedom for his sons; while she, to save them, must betray the cause he fought for. But a woman's children were dearer than freedom. "Oh, Lord," Linnet said, "what can a lone woman do?"

The tramp of marching men stilled suddenly and a fist banged on the door. Slowly Linnet opened it. There, in the first gray of dawn, red coats blazed against the snow.

A young officer addressed Linnet. "My men are hungry," he said. "Can you furnish breakfast for them?"

Linnet wrung her hands. "I've scarce enough corn ground for the young ones and for me."

"You've a samp mill in the garden. Put water on the fire and set to work."

Linnet stared at the old Indian mill as if she'd never seen its like before. "I'll grind it," she said at last, "if your men will pack corn from the attic."

She replenished the fire and waked the children, while British soldiers filed through her house, filling kettles and carrying corn. Eight-year-old Johnny rubbed his eyes and stared at the soldiers. "Hooray for the Republic!" he shouted.

Linnet whispered, "Hush, Johnny! They're British soldiers!"

"British soldiers? Then we got to shoot 'em, Ma!"

Linnet met the cold, merciless stare of the British officer. "You appeared so willing to feed my men, I took you for a Tory, ma'am."

"My husband is a Rebel sympathizer," Linnet faltered. "The—the young ones take after him."

He looked down at her with eyes that glinted like bayonet tips. "Get to your mill and grind the corn."

Linnet stood up, took little David on her arm, said, "Come, Johnny," and walked to the samp mill. The mill was a hollowed tree trunk set upright beside a sapling to which the heavy pestle was lashed. She banged the pestle down on the corn, the sapling jerked it back, and Linnet rammed it in again. She kept banging it down with fury in every stroke.

While soldiers scooped out the meal and refilled the tree

trunk, Linnet stood flexing her arms. Johnny watched with pure rage in his eyes.

Linnet reached for the pestle and a soldier said, "I'll spell ye, ma'am."

"And get my mill out of kilter!" Linnet snapped. "Thankee, no."

"You'll have little to grind but tree bark," he said, "when we are gone."

Linnet gasped, realizing for the first time that all her winter's corn could scarcely make two meals for such a company. She looked ahead at starvation and her hand faltered on the pestle, but she forced it down. "If only they don't burn the house."

The small winter sun blinked up, and still Linnet's arms swung up and down. Her back ached. Her head throbbed. Her every muscle screamed for rest. But she kept the pestle going. At the end the soldiers had to shove her away to scoop out the meal.

She staggered toward the house, but it was jammed with soldiers. They overflowed into the yard, eating half-cooked mush out of bowls and crocks and cups and mugs, even off of shingles. Three soldiers came up from the barn carrying a dozen hens by the legs. Others brought corn down from the attic and loaded their knapsacks. Sides of bacon and smoked hams hung over their shoulders. Pigs squealed, and Linnet knew they were being butchered to feed the British.

The officer gave a command, the men fell in, and marched away.

Linnet walked around the trampled yard, picked up the tatters of a liberty quilt which the soldiers had ripped to pieces. She found a wooden bowl the soldiers had dropped in the snow and searched the ground for scattered corn, gathering every precious grain.

Johnny said in a voice too old for him, " 'Twould serve us right if we starved—turning traitor like you did."

Linnet said, "Johnny, Johnny——" then broke off as gunfire clattered. A heavy volley roared out, then another and another. She dashed across the yard, sobbing, laughing, shouting, "She heard it! She heard it!"

Johnny asked, "Who, Ma? What?"

"Increase Rhodes. She's told me many a time she don't have to mark the days, for when she hears the samp mill going, it's Friday afternoon. And this is the Sabbath day.

I never ground corn on the Sabbath day, and I never ground corn afore sun-up."

"You mean she heard the mill off at the edge of town and warned the Continentals?"

"Yes, son. And if she listened close she knowed how many British was a-coming, for I hit each lot one hundred and four whacks when fifty would have ground it."

Johnny took her hand. "I—I'm purely proud, Ma."

" 'Twasn't much," Linnet said. "But what can a lone woman do?"

A DOWRY FOR WILLIE

Albert N. Williams

THIS is how Willie Fearless arranged for to get married to Gertrude Littleblood, a schoolteacher in North Platte, Nebraska, back in 1870.

Now there ain't nothing strange about a couple of people wanting to get married, then or now. However, a man shy as Willie Fearless, him even asking for a glass of water is mighty strange, so when he told us him and Gertrude was engaged, we nearly fell off our horses, me and Doughhead Charlie.

Yep, Willie was mighty, mighty shy. Used to cause him a lot of misery, account of his shyness made him nervous, and being nervous made him quick with his trigger finger. Folks used to call him unreasonable, the way he'd shoot first and ask questions later. Shucks, he wasn't unreasonable. He was just tongue-tied.

I always figgered Willie might loosen up once he got engaged to a girl, but no, sir, not so much as a howdy-do. It was so bad he made me and Doughhead do the bargaining with Gertrude's paw. "Shucks," says Willie, "I can't go dickering with a man about his daughter. Just ain't decent. I can buy and sell beef cattle, and trade mules and Indians, but it ain't right a man should bargain over women."

Well, Doughhead offered to make the arrangements. Now, Doughhead ain't much of a hand with the women himself —smells too high. But when it comes to striking a bargain, there just ain't no man in the States or islands can hold a candle to him. Why, he could talk an angel outen his harp, then stick him cartage for hauling it away.

'Course that's exactly what Willie wanted—someone who

could strike a good bargain. You see, getting married out there in the Old West wasn't like it is today. Then it was half love and half trading. First off a fellow'd decide if the girl's paw was anxious to get her off his hands. That took the calculation of a horse trader. However, if it turned out the girl was a liability, the chances were a good trader could lay claim to a few acres of good land and a team of horses to boot. Mules, at any rate. Dowry, they called it. Right sobering thought what some men'll do to get their daughters taken off their hands. Also a mighty sobering thought what some men'll go through to get their hands on a matched team of horses or a quarter-section of bottom land.

However, as far as Willie was concerned, there wasn't none of that worry, for Willie really loved this here Gertrude Littleblood. Told me so himself. And she was real purty, purty as a speckled hen. Little roan gal with a patch of red hair. Stood about as big as a dime's worth of liver, and appeared to come of good stock. Lived with her paw over the depot. Taught school, attended the Baptist Church, and probably would have voted straight Republican, had she been a man.

No, sir, there wasn't much chance of Willie getting beat down on that trade. But just the same, he was cautious, and he didn't want to take no chances in a situation where talking was required. That's why he asked Doughhead to do the dickering with Old Man Littleblood.

Doughhead, he thought the matter over, then said, "If I play my cards right, I'll get a team of mules to boot. I'll get the mules, even if I don't get the bride."

So we set off that afternoon to talk to Paw Littleblood. Paw kept a harness shop across the street from the drugstore, but spent most of his time down by Ed Spiteful's dram house, teasing and tickling the horses so they'd break their halters. Kept his business up to normal, so he said.

Now I hadn't never met Old Man Littleblood, having been in North Platte only about two weeks, but I'd heard about him. Appreciated a bargain's much as any man. Little more, if anything. Yep, he had quite a reputation around and about, and I could see that Doughhead was thinking the matter over as we rode down the street.

We stopped in front of the Oriental Laundry to ask a fellow some directions. "Looka here, neighbor," asked Doughhead, "do you know Old Man Littleblood?"

The stranger, who was resting, nodded. "Yes, I know Nate Littleblood."

"Where do you reckon we can find him?"

The fellow shifted his tobacco chunk. "Why, I don't know exactly," says he. "Was you to tell me your business, maybe I could help you."

Doughhead said, "Figger there is only one man who can help me, and that's Old Man Littleblood himself. I'm a-going to ask him for his daughter's hand for to get married with."

Now this here stranger was a long-connected sorta feller. 'Peared to come from kinda far down East. Pennsylvania way, or New York State, maybe. Didn't have much to say, but you could tell he was interested in passing events. "Who's making out to marry her?" he asked.

"Jest tell Old Man Littleblood that Willie Fearless is in town, and tooken a shine to his daughter."

"Willie Fearless," says the feller. "Huh. Now, what sort of a man is this here Willie Fearless?"

Doughhead sees he's got an audience, so he lets himself out. He settles back like a cow who's met a champeen milker. "Well, you can just tell folks that Willie Fearless is about the smartest, strongest, long-ridingest, sure-shootingest, cleanest-card-playingest soldier that ever got mustered outen the Tenth Illinois Regiment. Why, stranger, when the angel Gabriel calls in the bets up yonder, who do you think will be holding the four aces?"

The feller thinks a minute, then says, "General Grant?"

"Nope. Wrong you are. Grant's a good man, all right, but he don't measure up to my candidate, not by a stone's throw."

The feller thought another minute, then says, "Dan'l Webster?"

"Not a chance," says Doughhead. "Give you one more guess. There's only one man who can call hearts and spades when Gabriel sounds the call."

The feller all of a sudden brightened up and says, "You mean this here Willie Fearless?"

Doughhead beats his leg and shouts, "That's certainly right! Why, dog my cats if he ain't the man!"

THE stranger nodded his head. "H'mmm—that's mighty interesting. Tell me, this Fearless, does he spend much time in the card houses?"

"Willie Fearless in card houses? Why," says Doughhead, "he couldn't any more pass up a chance to lay a bet than you could pass up a chance to kick an Indian. Why, there ain't a faro dealer this side of St. Joe who don't know him better than his own mother."

The feller paused. "Gambling man, is he? Does he go often to the saloon?"

Doughhead just laughed. "Does a rabbit spend much time in a lettuce patch?"

"Quite a man, this here Willie Fearless, ain't he?" asks the stranger.

Doughhead, he leaned forward. "That's what you can tell your friend. He's quite a man. But tell me, does Old Man Littleblood own any property worth staking a piebald pony on?"

"Two hundred acres," says the feller.

"How far from the courthouse?"

"Courthouse is next to the property."

"How far from the railroad?"

"Railroad runs through the property."

"That right?" says Doughhead. "Mortgage on the property?"

The feller sneers, " 'Tain't likely. Littleblood don't believe in mortgages. They make him unhappy."

"H'mmmmm," says Doughhead. "Reckon a feller could do worse than marry up to this here daughter of Littleblood's."

"Feller could do a sight worse," says the man.

"Then I tell you what to do," says Doughhead. "Here it's getting late, and I got to start prospecting for some dinner. Got no time for to go looking for this Littleblood. Just you tell him what I said about Willie Fearless, and say that Willie would like to marry Gertrude."

Now that he'd done his duty, Doughhead sets back in his saddle preparatory to riding away, but the stranger stops him.

"Be happy to carry the message, neighbor," he says to Doughhead, "but do you want I should mention how interested you are in the land and property?"

"Lord, no," says Doughhead. "Willie, now that he knows the land is there, he'll really set out to get it, but you don't need to bring the matter up."

The old fellow sliced off a fresh piece of chomping tobacco. Doughhead was getting a wee mite impatient. "Looka here. How much argument do you think Littleblood will put up to this marriage?"

"Why, I don't think Nate Littleblood will offer much argument."

"That right?" says Doughhead.

"Nope. I don't think Littleblood will mind if his daughter can abide you. Far as the old man's concerned, he's got a lot of tolerance. And he's got a lot of admiration. Any man who'll bargain for a girl like she was government-brand beef, like you do, that man's got a future ahead of him. Specially when he don't try to pretend that he spends all his time in the Baptist Church after hours. Yep, a man that will proudly own up to card houses and dram houses, and even boast of his dealing skill, that's a man to back. A man that thinks only of land and cattle, he's miserly. Man that thinks only of women, he's lecherous and God'll smite him down. Man who thinks of both of them, he's a good man, and a man who'll help build up the territory out here. Man worth paying out some land to keep in North Platte. Yep, as far as this marriage goes, you can count it a bargain."

"A bargain? You'll shake hands on that?" says Doughhead.

"Yep, I'll shake on it."

Doughhead shook hands with the feller, and then turned to me. "You done witnessed the handshaking, Jack."

Yep, I'd witnessed the handshaking, and I writ X in the dust with my gun butt to seal the bargain. Then Doughhead spoke up once more. "Now looka here, mister, I'm powerful glad to have your sworn word that this here bargain is made, but how'll I know it will hold?"

"Don't worry about that," says the feller. "I know Nate Littleblood, and I can promise you it'll come off the way I said."

"How well do you know Littleblood?" asks Doughhead cautiously.

"Well, son," says the feller, smiling. "I am Nate Littleblood."

And that's how we got Willie Fearless accepted to Gertrude Littleblood's paw. Course we had to keep Willie in hiding until the ceremony took place, so's the old man wouldn't notice the difference between him and Doughhead, and then at the wedding we had to get the old man likkered up so he wouldn't notice the substitution. But once the marriage got under way, it turned out to be one of the biggest events that ever happened in Nebraska territory.

ACE HIGH

Ned Tomlinson

IN the beginning was hatred—deep, bitter, and, as is often the case, one-sided. Nobody in the mess knew the intensity of Henderson's feeling against Doyle, least of all, Doyle himself. Back in the States, before the war, they had attended the same college, and while Doyle had always been aware that Henderson's attitude was not particularly friendly, the man had been taciturn with everybody.

But here at the front, where things had a way of coming to the surface, the other officers sensed something they never put into words. Each concluded that maybe there was a point unsettled between the two. In time of war one does not inquire too closely into other men's affairs.

Henderson could have explained it if he had been called upon to do so—which he was not. It was nothing but jealousy; plain, stark jealousy; and deep down inside of him he knew it.

Doyle was a youngster of strong personal charm, full of laughter and the joy of living, while Henderson, lacking humor and the faculty of making friends, was the type of man who never could become popular.

In their college days Doyle was one of those gifted few who had been able to gain without effort or solicitation all those laurels so dear, and so vastly important, to undergraduate life. Henderson, who would have given his soul to have attained even a fraction of the success and popularity so carelessly won by the other, could only stand on one side, a sullen and lonely spectator.

And then, by some obscure mental process, Henderson began to picture Doyle as someone who had stolen these coveted things from him. He finally worked himself into a state of mind where he believed that if it had not been for the other, he, Henderson, would have made the track team; would have been on the staff of the college paper; would have made the smart senior society; would have had the prettiest girls of the season hanging on his arm at the commencement dance.

And so, in that fertile field of emotion that lies beyond the borderland of reason, hate was born. And its festering roots spread down into his heart, and poisoned his life.

They were thrown together again by some freak of chance, shortly after the United States entered the First World War, as junior officers of the Twenty-sixth Flying Squadron. Immediately all Henderson's old bitterness reawakened, and it was sensed by everyone except Doyle, whose overtures of friendship fell on barren soil.

Then one day the commander returned from headquarters with a more serious expression than usual.

"What's wrong, Cap?" someone called out. "Have they given you a month's leave?"

"Not exactly. They've handed us a bit, though, that will end by one of us going on a longer leave than that. All they want this time is a survey of Miramont—thirty miles behind the lines. A sweet rendezvous. The Hun ships will be like a swarm of hungry flies."

The other gave vent to a low whistle. "That's a job for a suicide," he said. "Who gets it?"

"According to my roster, it's between Henderson and Doyle," was the answer. "Ordinarily, I'd detail one of them, but this time it's sort of different. I'm going to let them decide for themselves."

And so it came about that these two stood on opposite sides of a card table: Doyle, smiling and nonchalant as usual; the other, pale and obviously nervous. It was Henderson, though, who spread the cards across, fanwise and face down.

"High man wins. Ace is high. Go ahead and cut," he said.

Doyle drew the ten of hearts.

There was a brief rustle among the little group of officers watching beside the table, then everything was still again.

Henderson reached out and, with a hand that seemed a trifle unsteady, turned over a card. It was an ace—the ace of spades.

"You go," he said quietly.

THREE miles high, and circling slowly, Henderson watched the drama unfold. Doyle had made his objective and was on his way back, with five German planes after him. He had outdistanced two, but two others were holding even, and blazing away at him not far behind. He might escape from them, but another and faster one, climbing rapidly, would be on his tail in a few minutes. And that would be the end of Doyle.

They were coming like arrows, but the shadow of death in that climbing German plane was traveling faster.

Alone in the rarefied atmosphere, one can see many things clearly. One's self, for instance. Perhaps that is what Henderson saw.

No one will ever know, for he did a strange and unexpected thing.

Considerably higher than the German, he suddenly opened his throttle, and came roaring down a steep incline with the speed of a bullet.

He made a perfect bull's-eye. Head on, he crashed into the Hun plane with such terrific force that both were torn asunder, and came fluttering down to earth in fragments, like an exploded shell.

Doyle just managed to make the American lines. He was helped out of the cockpit with two bullets in his shoulder and one in his right arm.

A mile or so back, in enemy territory, they picked up what was left of two airmen. A German officer, with characteristic thoroughness, was making an inventory of the contents of Henderson's pockets.

Among a few trifling odds and ends, he came across a pack of cards.

He was about to lay them aside with the other items, when something about them caught his eye.

He studied them intently, one by one, the faces and the backs. Then he grunted.

Walking over to an American soldier recently taken prisoner who happened to be standing near by, he held out the cards and said in English, with a sneer:

"See these? The cards are marked. The aces have little dots on the back. Your gallant airman was a crook."

The soldier, who had seen more of the air fight than the German, looked up into the clear blue sky.

"Maybe," he answered.

SCARED TO LIFE

Olga Rosmanith

GRAMP came to stay with us while his cottage got rebuilt, and Lightnin' came with him. Mom didn't want the big black dog, but Gramp was lonesome without him. "Lightnin's clean as folks," he said, "and better educated."

I wanted to pat him, but Mom held my shoulder. I went away with her back to the kitchen.

"No use getting attached, Billie," she said. "They won't be here long."

Gramp's cottage had burned while he was away fishing. He said he didn't mind, but it bored him living with us. "Where I live," he told me, "something allus is happening."

Thunderbird Valley, where we lived, was paradise to me. Our house was where the citrus groves ended and the desert began. There was a long cottonwood grove where the field workers lived—a row of cottages with yards swarming with goats, chickens, dogs, and babies.

Every morning Gramp said, "No gossip, no feuds, no fights—what a dull hole to live in!"

Mom just laughed at him. "It's lots of fun here," she said, "for folks with something to do."

"Too bad they don't do it," he said, "starting with this house."

He made a list for the hardware store and the mailman brought the package. Gramp whistled all over the house, repairing things for several days. Then all the windows fitted, the door handles turned, the floor boards stopped creaking, the bureau drawers slid in and out, the bulbs lit up and you could see the hanging switch-pulls in the dark.

After that, he taught Lightnin' to find where the setting hens hid their nests. He said you could teach the oldest dog new tricks if you knew the how of it. Mom came round to the idea that a dog could be clean, obedient, quiet, and good company. Gramp kept forgetting his Stetson if he took it off any place, and Lightnin' would go right back and get it for him. Mom finally agreed I could have a dog if Gramp would teach him good manners.

So Gramp went to the workers' cottages to look the pups over and find a likely one. "Lightnin's aren't born every day," he said. "Come on, Billie," he said, "you go with me."

There was a great commotion when we got there. They told Gramp they were scared stiff; they'd all seen a haunting. A gruesome shiny skull had gone past them last night, like it was floating.

Gramp began to whistle. At last something was going on. He said he couldn't just set in a chair at his age and watch the world go by. He wasn't a day over eighty yet. So he promised he would hunt this skull thing and catch it maybe. After that he went over to comfort the workers every night.

Mom was scornful, but she got curious and went once, while a neighbor stayed with me. She was awful quiet all next day.

Gramp went off for his walk and Lightnin' went with him.

"Mom," I said, "I want to see it. The boys up there see it every night. Why can't I see it?"

"Maybe there's nothing to see," she said, folding Gramp's blue shirt with the horseshoes on it. "A little imagination can put a lot of scare into folks."

Gramp returned, mopping his brow as usual.

"Any news of a dog for me?" I asked. I was worried the way Gramp refused one pup after the other.

"Maybe I'll ask round again tonight, when I go down to see if there's any more hauntings."

I didn't ask if I could go. I dressed again after Mom left me in bed and listened for Gramp to start out. Then I got out of the window on the porch and went after him.

"Gramp," I called, scared I would lose him when he turned into the cottonwood grove. "Gramp."

He waited for me and took hold of my hand when I got up to him. "You're shivering, son, and it's hot as hades. Ain't nothing to be scared about." But he didn't take me back to bed. "After all," he said, "a boy needs fun in his life."

The people were all outside Miguel Valdez' cottage, peering into the darkness. I got pins and needles in my stomach. I was afraid to see something and I was afraid to miss anything. One of the boys clutched me and then I saw it. A greenish, shiny skull came floating along in the dark and went on past us.

I threw myself in Gramp's arms and he held onto me. He was laughing. "Nothing to it, son. Some natural explanation."

After it vanished, we all went into Miguel's parlor. Gramp

had a drink and I had some little cakes with pink sugar on them. They talked and laughed and then they got out their guitars and began to play and sing. The field workers could make marvelous music.

When we got home, the house was dark and Mom was asleep. Lightnin' was lying on the step comforting his lonesomeness with Gramp's old Stetson between his paws. "That's a dog for you," said Gramp. "Never need a friend while a dog lies waiting."

Gramp had decided on a pup and we went for him next day. There wasn't much vacation left and I was so busy learning how to educate him to be almost folks, like Lightnin', I forgot all about the haunting. So it was like a terrible shock when I got haunted right in our own house.

ONE night after supper, Mom said, "Billie, go see if Gramp left the morning paper in his room." When I looked through the door, I saw the skull on his dresser, all made of greenish-yellow light.

I let out a scream like a fire siren. Gramp yelled, "Hold everything!" and came running. Lightnin' started barking and my pup howled like he wanted to go home to his mother.

Mom ran too, but Gramp got there first and turned on the light. There was nothing on the dresser but Gramp's old Stetson.

"Nothing here," he said to Mom. "The boy just had the heebie-jeebies."

He quick hid the little bottle of luminous paint he got from the hardware store to shine the light-pulls so we could see them in the dark. He saw me looking and gave me a long, slow wink. I thought of Lightnin' going in the dark to the rocks to get Gramp's hat where he'd been sitting, and going home with it past the cottonwoods—the black dog in the black night running with the hat in his mouth— and I laughed and laughed till the tears ran down my face and my sides were aching.

We had to tell Mom, and she said severely, "You're a bad man, Gramp, scaring those good, harmless people."

"But they liked it," said Gramp. "Half of them were sick when I came, bored to death with too much harmony."

Mother tried to look stern, but she began to smile a little. Gramp opened the kitchen door. "Listen," he said. "No haunting tonight, and nobody's making any music up there."

It was true, too. Then Mom began to laugh, and when she started there was no stopping her. If I hadn't had a dog growing up like Lightnin', I don't know what I would have done when Gramp and Lightnin' left.

"THOU SHALT NOT KILL"

Channing Pollock

"I DON'T understand you," the Reverend Peter Very declared. "If you're opposed to war——"

Harriet Quinner looked up from her knitting.

"There's no 'if' about that," she said. "I've been a member of every peace society ever formed in this town."

"Exactly," Mr. Very assented. He was a square-jawed, square-built little man, convinced that there were two sides to every question—his own and the wrong side. He had known "Miss Q." for years, and respected her. Everyone in this part of New England respected Miss Q. For generations her family had lived in the same white clapboard house and made its influence felt in every righteous movement.

"You agree with me that nations could and should settle their disputes as good citizens do——" went on the clergyman.

Miss Quinner nodded.

"——and yet you refuse to sign a petition calling upon our own country to disarm."

Miss Quinner was reversing her needles. Mr. Very had seen her do that hundreds of times, but still he couldn't help looking at her poor maimed left hand. Now his hostess followed his glance.

"I lost those fingers in Yucatán," she said.

"I know."

"I lost my sister there, too."

"Yes, I know that."

"She was all I had," Miss Quinner went on. "I've been alone ever since."

She rose and put down her work and crossed to the tall old-fashioned windows that faced the prim old-fashioned garden. She was a curiously quiet woman, Mr. Very thought. She reminded him of an ocean liner in a harbor—in a world full of panting, undecided tug boats.

Mr. Very waited a moment and cleared his throat and resumed. "Someone must lead the way," he said. " 'Thou shalt not kill.' Someone must show that there can be no excuse for murder."

He stopped because Miss Quinner so obviously was thinking of her own tragedy.

"I want to tell you how I lost my sister," she said. "No one else knows that."

"I had understood she was killed in a jungle."

"In the bush at Uxmal," Miss Quinner corrected him.

"That was just before I came here," Mr. Very remarked.

"It was something over ten years ago. The country really wasn't opened up yet, but Thompson had interested Harvard, and published a book or two. My sister and I had been in Egypt with my father before he died. I was anxious to compare the Egyptian ruins with those in Yucatán."

She returned to her chair but remained standing.

"I don't know why I took Florence. She was hardly more than a child, and very gay and romantic. I needed someone like that with me. We spent a week in a rest house at Chichén Itzá, and then we went back to Mérida, and engaged an Indian to take us to Uxmal. The man's name was Raymundo, and he drove a decrepit Ford from the end of the railway at Muna. We two women spent the night at Muna, and started for Uxmal at daybreak.

"It was frightfully hot, and the road was unbelievably bad. Florence and I were in the back seat of the Ford, and Raymundo sat in front with a double-barreled shotgun beside him. Florence asked him why he had brought that. He said he wanted to kill pigeons."

"What did he do with them?" Mr. Very asked.

"I don't know. Ate them, I suppose, or sold them. But I was horrified. I love birds. I used to be president of our Audubon Society. So I argued with Raymundo, and then tried to buy him off. I suppose he thought I was crazy. Anyway, he brought down one dove from the car. The poor little thing; it wasn't even dead yet. Florence cried, and I was furious, but Raymundo only laughed and reloaded his gun."

Mr. Very inclined his head. He'd heard an outline of the story before, and he was anxious to get his petition signed and go home to dinner. Miss Quinner picked up her knitting and sat down with it in her lap.

"It was noon when we reached Uxmal," she continued, "and no shade anywhere. Just bush and half-buried heaps of stone and a blistering sun. Raymundo said there was a big tree half a mile through the bush. He began carrying our lunch there, and Florence wandered off, and I waited alone in the car. And then Raymundo came back for us and his gun and the dead pigeon, and I told him I'd rather starve than eat that. He laughed again, and we all went into the bush and had bread and a native dish of beans and some fruit. There was a cool breeze there, and Raymundo dozed off. So did Florence.

"I was nodding myself when suddenly I saw a queer movement in the bush. I touched Raymundo's arm and pointed and whispered, 'What's that?'

"Raymundo listened, and then whispered back:

" 'Wildcat.'

"An instant later the beast broke cover. Raymundo reached for his gun."

Miss Quinner looked down again at her maimed hand.

"He was too late, I suppose?" Mr. Very remarked sympathetically.

Miss Q. shook her head.

"His aim was bad, then?"

"I don't think so," Miss Quinner said. "He was a dead shot. But my sister was killed—almost torn to pieces. And my arm and hand were torn too. The beast was half starved. Raymundo had to club him off."

"I don't understand," Mr. Very repeated himself. "If the Indian was a dead shot, and the gun was loaded——"

"It wasn't," Miss Quinner interrupted, suddenly upright in her chair. "The gun wasn't loaded. I knew that. I knew it before I heard the hammers click on two empty chambers. I'd taken the shells out while I was alone in the car so Raymundo couldn't kill pigeons."

Miss Quinner's voice had become shrill.

And then, very quietly, she picked up her knitting.

"I've never told anyone else," she concluded.

Mr. Very rolled up his petition.

"You were right to tell me," he said.

LET 'EM EAT FRUITCAKE

Sid Schumann

IT's not I'm a crab. It's not I'm agin managers. There's prob'ly some managers beat their wives only once a week. Maybe less'n that. Prob'ly don't even use whips. Could be.

But there's guys! Now like you take the time I had this stock-clerk job in Los Angeles, right across from Westlake Park.

It's a West Coast drugstore I'm workin' in and it has about fifty in help, includin' Donovan, the pharmacist. It's not a bad place to work. I like the job and I like the store. Come lunch hour, we had that park where you could get some sun and chew the fat with the cosmetics girls. I'm really startin' to enjoy life when we get a new manager one morning who wears rubber soles and is called Elmer Craven.

He looks harmless, and we're watchin' him all day to see if he's gonna like us or we're gonna like him or vice versa. We notice when he wants something done he don't come straight out. That don't seem to be his way. He'll sorta ooze over and kinda go into a conference with whoever he's aimin' to talk to. "Don't you think, Mr. Taylor," he'll say "—don't you think we ought to display the gopher traps where the turkey fryers used to be?" Or he'd say, "I wonder if the rayon panties would look better in Feminine Hygiene?" He never expected but what you'd agree. We wouldn'a' minded if he'd come clean and tell us what to do.

Once a manager starts usin' psychology, you're sunk. It wasn't a month but what he had Drugs tearin' its hair, Liquor bitin' its nails, Cosmetics developin' the jerks, and a first-class underground movement brewin' in Sundries.

Anyway, our warehouse truck rolls up one morning with two huge cases of what the driver swears is lead. I finally manages to get the cases inside the store, when one of them splits. I stick my hand in and take out a square, soft, dark brown, heavy slab' of somethin' wrapped in cellophane. It's got a bright-colored label on it which says: "Grandma's Old English Fruitcake, net weight 2½ lbs."

"Oh, golly," says Miss Jones from Cosmetics. She comes over, picks one up, and smells it. "I think," she says, looking up "—I think it has eggs in it."

"One hundred and forty-four pieces," says the Liquor girl. "Poor Grandma musta stayed up all night."

From Drugs I hear, "One fruitcake—one generous bottle of rhubarb and soda—both for ninety-eight cents!"

Craven finally soft-shoes over. "Don't you think——" he starts conferencin'. But I'm way ahead of him. "You're right," I says. "We'll display eighteen cakes in each department." And I proceeds to distribute.

In a way, I guess I'm lucky I don't have to sell stuff. But even I can see, after a bit, that Grandma isn't movin' too spry. The first week Cosmetics sold one cake. The second, Feminine Hygiene sold two, but had one returned. The third week Liquor gets a four-bit deposit on one, but the customer later backs out. Craven's gettin' a bit worried. It's a "distribution" and it's no feather in his cap if he returns the lot. After all, Craven wants to be known as a "tight operator," which is the highest compliment the office can bestow on a manager who moves his merchandise fast. So he tries a new tack.

"Miss Jones," he says one morning, "don't you think it would be better *not* to remind each customer about the fruitcake, but simply pick it up after you've sold a lipstick and say casually, 'I must remember to take one of these home'? Suggestion is usually very effective—don't you think?"

Actually everybody in Number Five is tryin' to sell those fruitcakes the best and quickest way they know. In the first place, they're takin' up too much room, besides which the cellophane is startin' to crack and the cakes are be-ginnin' to look kinda haggard from bein' picked up casually a hundred times a day, pinched, weighed, smelled and put down—gently but firmly.

THE guy who is maddest of all is Donovan the pharmacist, and ever since I can remember he's always squawked about the stuff they kept puttin' on his prescription counter, like turtles, bean pots, and light fuses. And now he's got these eighteen chunks of fruitcake starin' him in the face.

The thing finally comes to a head. We're takin' inventory, and we find we still got one hundred and thirty-eight cakes strewn all over the store and no relief in sight. Fact is we mighta gotten rid of them on Fountain, but the fountain manager says no soap. "I built up too good a trade," he explains. So now Elmer comes out with his sixty-four-dollar suggestion, which is that every clerk buy two cakes at the discount price of eighty-nine cents apiece. This would reduce the stock to thirty-eight slabs, which would then be crated and consigned back to Commissary, where they came from.

So when we hear we're gonna be taxed almost two dollars—adding insult to indigestion by havin' to take home them cement patties—we're really fit to be tied. There is no good way we can get out of it—except, of course, to quit. We're mad—mad as blazes. And Donovan is the maddest.

He comes out of his cage while Craven's doin' somethin' down the cellar. "You guys buyin' them cakes?" he asks the bunch. And before you get a chance to answer, he adds, "Now, look. You can buy 'em, if you like, but promise me this."

"What?" we asks.

"Promise me you'll hold off till payday."

Payday's Saturday—just two days off—so we promise. "What are you figurin' to do?" I asks Donovan.

"I'm going to make Craven remember fruitcake as long as he lives!"

WELL, Saturday morning comes and we're all waitin' outside the store for Craven to come to open up. It's seven thirty, then eight. At eight fifteen I puts in a call. Craven ain't there, so I get the assistant, Trunnell, on the phone, and in an hour we open for business.

That was the last any of us ever saw Craven again! Monday, I wrapped up those mortician muffins and back to Commissary they went.

Well, you know about me leavin' the West Coast outfit to join the Marines, and it isn't till a year later, when I'm back with a medical discharge, and me and Miss Jones—who's been transferred to Number Fourteen—are having a quiet drink in a bar on Sunset Boulevard. We look up and who should we see but Mr. Elmer Craven, big as life.

"Hello, Mr. Craven," I says and I invites him over to our table. He greets us by our right names, which shows he remembers, and sits down. We orders and I'm sittin' there dyin'! I nudges Jones.

"Mr. Craven," she asks, "whatever happened to you down at Number Five? It's over a year and no one ever found out what became of you."

"Well, Miss Jones, it's a long story. You remember that Saturday morning I failed to open up? I became very sick during the night. In fact, I was forced to go to the hospital. They had to pump my stomach and I did feel better after that. They found nothing unusual, which was, of course, very puzzling."

"You mean you don't know what made you sick?" I asked.

"No. The peculiar part is that I cannot, since that happened, stand the smell of a drugstore. It makes me deathly uncomfortable. I've had to leave the drug business."

I HAD an impulse I couldn't resist. "What became of Donovan?"

Craven looks at me, then at Jones and then at his drink. "Funny," he says. "Funny you should be asking me. I've often thought of Mr. Donovan. It does seem to fit in so well—and yet I could never make certain," he says.

"Certain of what?" I asks.

"That Friday," he says, leanin' closer, "I was extraordinarily busy all afternoon. Something went wrong with Mr. Donovan's register and it kept me for almost two hours before I could get it into operation again. Then there were some mistakes in his cash and we had to total the detail paper. Well, it wasn't until eight o'clock that I was able to sit down at the fountain for a bite to eat. There was nothing worthwhile left. Mr. Donovan took one of the fruitcakes we had on display. You remember, I suppose—"

"Yeah," we both said, "we remember."

"He had intended to buy two of them anyway and he thought he'd treat me to some of his. I had never really tasted those cakes. I ordered a malt with two eggs—I was quite hungry. I ate the fruitcake and drank the malt while Mr. Donovan rested and smoked and talked. It's quite an interesting life Mr. Donovan's led. I was so engrossed that I found I had eaten almost a whole cake." Craven sets his drink down and looks out into the street. Then he adds, "I've often wondered if it wasn't that cake that caused my illness."

"I wonder where Donovan is," says Craven later. "He was a rather fine chap."

"Yep," I says, at the same time holdin' on to Jones so she doesn't roll off her chair. "Donovan sure was a swell egg. Would you say, Craven," I adds, deadpan, "would you say Mr. Donovan was what you'd call a tight operator?"

A CUP OF WATER

Albert Payson Terhune

THE snort of a horse had made Kirby glance up from the sweatful task of pumping a new-patched tire tube. He had left his crazy car's engine running, lest it refuse to start afresh.

Thus he had not heard the soft padding of unshod hoofs over the sandy ground.

Some fifty lean men sat their leaner mounts, staring in stolid curiosity at the chugging machine. (Automobiles were a startling rarity to the Bedawi of the Moab country in those prewar days.)

A hawk-faced oldster walked his horse out from the half circle. Kirby straightened, touched his brow and breast in salutation, and strove to give courteous indifference to his tone as he said:

"*Naharak sa-id* [May your day be happy], Sheik Ysouf!"

Kirby knew the Near East too well to augur anything favorable from the idle exchange of compliments which followed.

Born in his father's mission house near Nablus, he had lived in Syria until he was sent to America to college and to engineering school. Then the Cabell Company had sent Kirby to the land of Moab to manage its little Transjordan antimony mine in the foothills under Nebo.

"Kirby *howaji*," Ysouf was saying, "the black camel has knelt at the door of El-Kanah. Two nights agone my own kinsman, Beni-Diab, was slain. The dirge still sounds for him."

"*Ohé!*" chanted Kirby, in the same singsong drone. "*Alhandulillah!* May he lie where rose leaves shall fall upon his tomb! Beautiful and tall was Beni-Diab, even as the——"

"Beni-Diab was shot dead outside your tent, at the mine whose sheik you are!" Ysouf broke in harshly upon the civil mourning chant. "He——"

"Allah has deprived of wisdom and truth the madman who told you such a lie, *effendi!*" exclaimed Kirby with much indignation. "True, a man was slain there, as you say. But not a noble of El-Kanah's tribe. It was a filthy night prowler. The guard saw him creep out of my tent in the darkness, carrying the canvas bag which held the laborers' pay. The guard fired and the *fellaheen* thief fell. When we came with lanterns, some accomplice had dragged the body away. I am but just returning from the serail, where I went to report the affair. You can realize the shot man could not have been Beni-Diab, since he was a sneaking tent thief. Surely no kinsman of the illustrious——"

"We waste time," interposed Sheik Ysouf. "You know the law."

Yes, Kirby knew to the letter the blood-atonement law of the Bedawi. As manager of the Cabell mine, he himself was responsible for the killing of the Bedouin night thief and must pay the debt.

At a signal from Sheik Ysouf, fifty or more slugs from the long-barreled flintlocks would rip through him where he stood. There would be no witnesses on this spot of desolation.

On his way here, his car had passed a half troop of irregular pashalic Turkish cavalry on its way back to the barracks, south of Zoar's site. The captain, a lifelong acquaintance of his, had hailed him in good-fellowship.

The cavalry could not be far behind him. At sight of these immemorial foes, the outlaw Bedawi would scatter like dust before the sirocco. But—

"I am parched with thirst and dust," whined Kirby cringingly, as Sheik Ysouf turned in his saddle to give the firing signal. *"Effendi,* by your creed, my throat must parch in hell through all eternity. By your guest right, you may not refuse a cup of water to foe or to brother. I ask a gourdful from the goatskin bottle at your crupper. By your own sacred guest-right, I claim it."

Impatient of the delay, Sheik Ysouf poured water from the goatskin into the gourd cup which hung beside it.

"Drink!" he bade the prisoner. "But drink swiftly."

Kirby took the cup and lifted it toward his lips. Then he lowered it and peered in fright over his shoulder at the tensely waiting tribesmen.

He raised his eyes beseechingly to Ysouf's scornful gaze.

"Drink?" he quavered. "And be shot or stabbed in the back while yet I am drinking? No. Among your men there are those who gladly would rob me of that last moment of joy for the blood feud's sake. Thus was your people's foe, Abou Hussein, struck down while he drank. I——"

"You shall not be slain as you drink!" declared Ysouf, his face contracting at this reminder of the one recorded blot on the guest-right's sacredness. "I swear it, for my men and for myself, on the spirit of Beni-Diab."

"Am I a three-day passenger at Jaffa, to think such an oath would hold, made to an unbeliever like myself?" stammered Kirby, cringing lower, yet his voice rising almost to a scream. "If indeed you and yours will let me drink my last draft in peace, then swear to me by the triple oath which no man may break—even to an unbeliever—and hope to look upon the face of Allah the Compassionate. Swear I shall not be slain or harmed until I have drunk this cup empty. I call on you in the guest-right's name."

Now, the triple oath, odd as its terms may seem to a foreigner, is one not to be taken lightly. But neither is an implication that the holy guest right may be violated.

Intoning as if in prayer, Sheik Ysouf called loudly:

"You shall take no hurt from me or from mine until you have drunk empty the cup you hold. I swear it—on the sword of the Prophet, on the beard of my father, on the milk of my mother. *Tamám!*"

With the speed of light, Logan Kirby tossed the contents of the gourd high into the air. The water cascaded earthward. The sandy ground sucked it in as it fell.

"*Khater-karak* [Thanks], O brother to eagles!" laughed Kirby, his semblance of craven cowardice falling from him. "Bid your riders find for me the water which my awkwardness spilled, and return it drop by drop to the gourd, and I will drink it. Until then, by your oath, I shall take no hurt from you or yours. *Mashallah!*"

In the instant of blank silence, the still air brought to Kirby's ears the jingle of cavalry equipment and a multiple tread of hoofs from beyond the bend of the road. His taut nerves relaxed.

He battled against an overmastering desire to sit down on the ground and cry.

BACK IN TOWN

Frederick Nebel

HARRY BARR'S insides began to tighten as the bus neared town. He knew where it would make its regular stop—in front of Sully's Drugstore. He could see the long green bench under the awning. People he had known all his life would be sitting on the bench, and he'd get off there, his eyelids narrowed, his eyes seeing at once nothing and everything. He'd walk up Main Street past the stores, past the people hanging out in front of them. He'd see old MacDonald sitting in front of the haberdashery. But he wouldn't look at MacDonald, or speak to him.

Already, knowing the town was so near, beyond the next turn, Harry's heart began to pound. He rose and said, "Let me off at the turn, will you?"

He stood in the summer dust of the road's shoulder and watched the bus disappear round the turn. Fifty feet up the road he found the path and entered the woods. It was the long way—two miles longer—but he would not have to run the gantlet of the townspeople.

When he reached the edge of the woods that bordered his folks' place, he wished he had ridden into the town, walked up Main Street. He knew with burning clarity that something fine and resolute had been almost within his grasp and he had let it go.

His father stood in the chicken-house doorway. Harry stopped and nodded toward the garden.

"Sure looks nice, Pa."

His father gazed at the garden for almost a minute. Then he came over to where Harry stood and they both gazed at the garden. His father put his hand on Harry's shoulder.

"Boy," he said slowly. "Boy."

He kept patting Harry's shoulder in a fond, almost absent-minded way. His mouth, under its gray, untidy mustache, was quirking. Then all at once it was still; and his hand, after one long squeeze, was still too.

"Go see your ma, Harry. She's on the front porch." The old man peered toward the woods. "She was looking for you to come by the street."

As his father turned toward the chicken house, Harry thought he saw a shadow of concern cross his face. Harry moved along the side of the house to the front porch.

His mother stopped rocking in the old Boston rocker. She got up with a kind of grave wonder in her face. She took him by the arm and led him inside, into the parlor. She sat down on the sofa and pulled him down beside her. She kept hold of his arm with both hands and he could feel her small, strong fingers digging into his flesh. The tears began to roll down her cheeks.

"There, Ma," he said. "There, now. Gee, look at you, all dressed up and everything. I saw Pa out back. Pa looks fine."

"You're back," his mother said, holding onto his arm. "You're back, Harry."

HE was back. For the first time in six months he slept in his own bed and wakened to see white curtains blowing in the morning breeze. He was back—but it wasn't the same. It was the same at home, but beyond his home—in the next street, in the village—was public opinion.

"Mister," the warden had said, "you have paid your debt to society. Believe me, it's my sincerest hope that the society to which you are now returning will realize that. But you, too, will have to do your part." MacDonald, too, had spoken of his debt to society. "Returning the money," MacDonald had said, "is not enough. The tax money was in his trust. He used the money. As a citizen and taxpayer of this town, I demand that he be tried in a court of law and, if convicted, sentenced to repay, in prison, his debt to society."

There was always, when Harry thought of it, a dreamlike quality about his taking the money. He had intended only to use the three hundred dollars over the long Labor Day weekend. As clerk in the tax collector's office, he had had access to the safe; and with the tax collector away at the time, it had been easy. The automobile salesman had driven the sixty miles from Portland, arriving Friday afternoon.

Short of cash, Harry asked him if he couldn't hold the deal off until Tuesday, but the salesman said the car had to be taken that day and a substantial down payment made. Harry had waited so long for a car that, with one at his fingertips, he was at his wits' end. Then he thought of the money in the safe. He took it, planning to drive to Portland Tuesday morning, cash some government bonds he had in a safe-deposit box there, and be back in town with the money by noon. But on the way to Portland he had skidded and cracked up. Taken to a hospital, he had been in a semiconscious state for almost a week—and in the meantime the loss of the tax money had been discovered.

"Son," his father had said, "you did wrong."

"I know, Pa."

"Your credit's always been good in town, the way a man's has got to be in a small town."

"I know, Pa. I did wrong. But George MacDonald——"

"George MacDonald is a hard man but a just one. When you were making only fifteen dollars a week, George MacDonald was the first man to run a charge account for you. And who has credit with George MacDonald can get credit anywhere else in town. But when you play free with taxpayers' money, then George MacDonald is your enemy."

For the first time in six months Harry went downstairs to his mother's breakfast. Here, at any rate, he felt safe, secure. His father talked desultorily, in his laconic way, about housing and how hard it was to get materials. His father was a carpenter.

"If you get into town today, Harry, get me some razor blades, will you?"

But Harry didn't go into town. He worked in the garden, repaired the fence that surrounded it. When his father asked about the razor blades next day, Harry said he hadn't gone in, and his father gave him a sober sidewise look. His mother got them that afternoon.

Harry was not lazy. He put a coat of paint on the barn, looked after the chickens, the pigs, the cow. One day, when he was repairing a screen on the front porch, he saw the mailman, Mr. Dow, up the street. He laid down the screen and went indoors until the mailman had passed by.

"What you planning, boy?" his father said a couple of weeks later. "No one means to push you—this is your home— but——"

Harry saw it there before him in the Portland paper. "They're looking for men upcountry, Pa. Cleaning out timber. I was planning to leave tomorrow."

Harry boarded the bus at the northern edge of the township next morning and rode it up into the mountains and through the mountains to the wild country near the Canadian border. He signed on for work and nobody asked him any personal questions. He went deep into the woods. The sense of freedom he felt was so wonderful that he suffered the rigors of the work without complaint. His body toughened up. His mind, bit by bit, day by day, cleared. He could go on forever in this freedom, moving from job to job.

But he couldn't forget his folks. He couldn't forget the bare gray tone of resignation in his father's voice. And always the town was in the back of his thoughts; and at the center of the town, like a hub at the center of countless spokes, was old man MacDonald. By the end of two months he knew that his new-found freedom was an illusion.

HE went back. Hard and brown, quiet, watchful, he rode the bus down into the center of the town. He knew now that the gantlet had to be run. If ever he were to bring any comfort to his folks, or a measure of peace to himself, he would have to face the town. The bus was held up by a traffic block in front of MacDonald's haberdashery. Harry, with his heart in his throat, stepped out and walked straight across the sidewalk. MacDonald was sitting on a chair outside the store.

"Hello, Mr. MacDonald," Harry said politely.

MacDonald gave him a cool, contemplative appraisal. He rose unhurriedly and followed Harry into the store.

"I'd like a couple of white shirts," Harry said.

MacDonald said, "Size fifteen, thirty-four sleeve."

Harry kept his hand in his pocket, clenched on a roll of bills—over two hundred dollars. "Some socks," he said, "brown, gray."

"Size eleven."

Harry chose six pairs. He picked out two ties and three sets of underwear, and all the while his hand worked at the money in his pocket. He could hardly wait to take it out.

"I guess that's all for now," he said. "How much?"

There was a thump on the counter. Harry saw old MacDonald open a long thumb-indexed ledger and turn the pages to B. Fascinated, he watched MacDonald enter the items in the ledger under the name Barr, Harry. His own name. In the charge-account ledger.

"Comes to twenty-two forty," MacDonald said.

Harry had not taken the money out of his pocket. Gradually his fingers relaxed. When he withdrew his hand, it was empty, the palm damp with sweat.

MacDonald wrapped everything in one large bundle and slid it across the counter. "Come in again, Harry," he said, and went to the back of the store to drink a glass of water.

With the bundle under his arm, Harry reached the sidewalk. He gave a small, nervous laugh. His throat was full. He was back in town—really back—for the first time. He wasn't afraid any more.

"Hey!" he called out. "Hey, Mr. Dow, you going my way?"

Mr. Dow, the mailman, braked his car sharply in the middle of the street. "Sure thing, Harry. Come on, hop in."

SHORT DRINK

Ray Nafziger

THE first car along the hot, spongy highway carried the homesteader widow who ran the filling station in Mescal Canyon. Plainly she hadn't driven across the Tecolote Mountains a few hours before to murder old Tom Wall for his eight hundred dollars of cattle money, but Henry Bayliss, obeying sheriff's orders, waved her down and glanced over the tires.

Whoever had shot Tom Wall at his ranch on the east slope

of the Tecolotes had parked on the highway and walked to the house. Unless the fresh shoe tracks and one smooth tire print just off the pavement lied.

"Tom Wall's killer is clear outa Arizona by now," the woman said above the violent boiling of her car. "Must of been the party that drove lickety-split past my oil station 'fore daylight. The cougar hunters camped at my place said it was a open roadster. You're wastin' time here."

"Likely," admitted Henry. "Your radiator acts clogged with gyp deposit; that Mescal Canyon water is chock-full of alkali." His mouth was dry as an old adobe brick. "You don't happen to be carryin' anything to wet a dry throat, ma'am?"

The woman glared and drove on.

"She thought I meant whiskey, I guess," Henry muttered and mopped his bristle-studded face.

Cars were few. An hour brought only the mail carrier and an oil truck. Another hour; and the sheriff whipped up in his battered sedan.

"You might as well go home," he told Henry. "The snake that killed old Tom is a long ways off by now."

"Lord, but I'm dry!" growled Henry Bayliss. "And nobody passin' here carries any water."

"Why should they, travelin' a paved highway?" The sheriff knew that Henry was thirsty mainly because he was harking back to the days when he and Tom Wall had ridden this dry, hot range together. "Tom sort of raised you, didn't he?"

"He took me in charge when I was left a range orphan. Summers him and me rode this Tecolote country after Tex King's longhorns."

"Heard that you two near died of thirst in here once," said the sheriff. Talking would be good for Henry.

"Yeah. These blasted Tecolotes a'most ended us. I guess they got about the least and worst water of any place on earth. The springs at the quicksilver mine would poison a goat and there's other water so evil-flavored one drop ruins a gallon of coffee. But that time the 'Paches raided through here, we would of sold our souls for one swallow of the worst of all those waters."

A truck loaded with ore labored up the hill and passed.

"Tom and me was a'ready thirsty when we had to hide out from them copperskins on the desert east of the Tecolotes. My horse give out and with my tongue bloated big as a washtub I went plain crazy. Tom was near done for too, but he'd roped me on his saddle and staggered along afoot, leading us into the Tecolotes.

"When Tom fetched up at a spring under a cliff—one we'd never run across—it was a miracle, like Moses making water spout from a rock. I was plumb gone but Tom brung me round, moistenin' my black and swole-up tongue at first and dippin' water over me. And what water! Good and sweet and cold. We laid there a whole day, soakin' ourselves inside and out. Then all a sudden Tom got up and begun layin' out squares with stones. I figgered he'd gone loco——"

An old touring car ground up the hill, dragging a trailer with a saddled horse. Buck Persons, who trapped coyotes and hunted mountain lions for the bounty, was driving. His fourteen-year-old son, Lonnie, sat on a bedroll in the back. Two carsick hounds had their heads stuck out of the right front window.

"Got that bearing put in a hour ago, sheriff," Buck Persons said, "and decided to pull out for home. Too hot and dry on the west side them Tecolotes for the hounds to keep a trail, and with the car busted all week, we couldn't git over to try the east slope."

"Just as hot and dry over on the east slope anyway," said Henry Bayliss, glancing up from Persons' set of new six-ply tires. His eyes went back to the horse in the trailer. "Well, look at that. Some folks still got enough sense to carry water."

He strode back to reach eagerly for the canteen hanging from the saddle horn. After one swallow, he carefully screwed on the cap again.

"You didn't git over on the east slope, Buck?" he said slowly from the side of Persons' car.

"Nope. Lonnie and me aimed to, but we been waitin' all week at the Mescal Canyon oil station for a bearing. It come just this morning."

"But you had a horse," said Henry. "He looks a mite ga'nted. Sure you didn't ride him 'cross the mountains last night, Buck?"

The hunter answered with a bluff promptness: " 'Course not. What would I do that for?"

"For to get eight hundred dollars. You rode over the range to hit the highway near Wall's ranch and tied the horse. Then you walked on down the pavement to leave tracks between the highway and Wall's house. And used a piece of old casing to make a smooth tire print in the dust so folks would figure the killer come in a car. Cuss you!" exploded Henry, and reached in to clamp his fingers around Buck Persons' throat.

In the back seat, Lonnie lifted a revolver from his lap. The sheriff jumped and joggled the boy's arm, so that the shot sailed wide. Then he disarmed Lonnie and pried Henry's big hands off Buck's throat.

Obeying a hunch, the sheriff explored a hole in a seat cushion and found a wad of bills. Grimly he counted eight hundred dollars.

"Didn't need that money for proof," said Henry. "Buck filled up this canteen at Tom's spring. Ridin' back in the mornin' cool, Buck only half emptied it. I knowed Buck killed Tom soon's my tongue touched that water. After all the thirstin' I done in this country, I could tell from one taste where any Tecolote water come from, but specially any from Tom Wall's spring.

"That was the same water Tom found that time we near cashed in. Like I was tellin' you, sheriff, after we'd laid a day drinkin' from that spring, Tom begun markin' out squares with stones. I thought he'd gone loco, but he hadn't.

" 'These is rooms of the house I'm buildin',' Tom Wall told me. 'Here, beside the only water in these Tecolotes that's sweet and good and fit to drink. This is where I'm settlin', to live my life here, drinkin' this good sweet water until I die.' "

EXIT FOR A HERO

Gerald Mygatt

FREDDIE paled as his father talked on the telephone. He looked as if he were going to be sick. His father hung up and, turning to Freddie, said, "The vet can take him now. Want to go down with me, old man?"

"No," said Freddie between clenched teeth.

"I wish you would, Freddie. You can sort of hold him while I drive. It—it isn't very easy for me either, you know. After all, Cap really belongs to all of us."

"Yes, but just the same he's mine," said Freddie. "Look, Dad—just one more day. Can't we wait till tomorrow?"

His father said, "We've waited too long as it is. The dog is suffering terribly. You know that as well as I do."

"I suppose so," said Freddie. And then he said, "The vet.

He might be scared of the vet. That would be awful—to end up scared."

"That's one reason why I want you there."

"Oh," said Freddie.

"The vet knows how to do it, son. He's done it for hundreds of dogs. He did it for the Carpenters—remember?—only a couple of months ago. He just gives them a whiff of chloroform and it's all over."

"I chloroformed a cat once," Freddie said soberly. "With Tot Lawrence. We used a garbage pail, and the cat just fought and fought. Pretty near pushed the cover off. It was fierce. I had to sit on the cover, and then I couldn't stand it any more and I yanked the cover off. But the cat was as good as dead by then. Anyway, he died. I wouldn't want Cap to have chloroform, Dad."

"They have different ways, Freddie. We could ask him for something different."

"Hooey!" said Freddie. "They tell you they'll use something different, but chloroform's cheap, I guess. The vet will give us a lot of baloney, and then he'll use chloroform anyway."

"The kindest thing, of course," said Freddie's father "—the kindest thing would be a gun. But we haven't got a gun. Even if we had one, I don't believe I'd have the nerve to pull the trigger. Not on Cap. You wouldn't either, Fred."

"N-n-no," said Freddie, going very white again. "I—no, Dad, I wouldn't."

"Well, might as well face it," said Freddie's father, shrugging. "I'll get the car out of the garage. You bring Cap out when I blow the horn. Better carry Cap. It's painful for him to walk."

The moment his father left the house Freddie dashed upstairs. He had, perhaps, two minutes. He meant to use them. For one thing he *had* a gun. It was a shotgun; pretty seedy-looking, but it worked. He had got it from Walt Bannister through a slick trade: his microscope, plus a real German helmet which Freddie didn't want because he had two, and a piece of a Jap flag. Since Freddie was only just twelve, he hadn't yet dared tell his father and mother about the gun; he figured on leading up to that gradually. But now it didn't matter. He had the gun. He had five shells for it. He would put Cap out of his misery—as his father had said—the kindest way. Just simply take Cap out in the woods behind the house and then over the hill, and start to talk to Cap, and then bang-o! He would argue the gun out with his father later.

Did he have the nerve to do it? His father might not have, but he had. Anything to keep Cap away from that stinking chloroform.

Freddie paused to make sure that his mother was out of the way. Yes, he could hear her humming in her bedroom. The rest was very easy. The shells were in his pocket by now. The gun—a quick run downstairs and the gun was outside, tucked into a corner by the grape arbor. It was dusk, growing dark, perfect for ducking away.

Freddie's father blew the horn. That meant he had the car backed out of the garage. Freddie moved fast. Cap was in the kitchen, of course. Nowadays he was always in the kitchen, lying beside the electric stove that years ago had been a coal stove, and cozily warm. It must have been all the same to Cap—an imaginary warmth. Or else Cap was eternally hopeful that the coal stove would be put back. Freddie didn't know.

Cap whimpered a little when Freddie picked him up in his arms. That would be Cap's pain.

"We're going out in the woods," said Freddie to Cap. "Just like the old days. Hey, Cap?"

Cap stretched around and licked Freddie's face. He licked it warmly. "We got to go," said Freddie, and let himself and Cap out of the kitchen door. At the corner by the grape arbor he stooped and picked up the gun.

CAP was a very old dog. He had been an old dog since Freddie could remember. He was a big dog too. Black, as black as coal. Nobody—much less Cap—had any idea as to who, or what, his father might have been. Cap's mother had been a sort of mixture. So Cap was doubly a mixture, which was just fine with Cap. Everything was fine with Cap, particularly having his ears fooled with by Freddie.

After about an eighth of a mile through the woods, Freddie, who was panting, set the gun and Cap down. He found a log, squatted on it. Immediately Cap shoved his long head between Freddie's knees. That was Cap's manner of saying that he wanted his ears tousled. Freddie tousled them. Then he picked Cap and the gun up again and climbed the hill, where they couldn't hear the gun from the house, or not very much.

"You're heavy," said Freddie to Cap, breasting the hill. Cap again stretched around and licked Freddie's face.

"Have a heart," said Freddie.

Cap had a heart. He licked Freddie's face some more.

"Quit it," said Freddie. Cap quit it.

Freddie fought through the briers till he got to an open place. He eased Cap down. He eased the gun down.

"Look, Cap," said Freddie, "you got to back off a ways." Freddie put a shell in the gun, threw off the safety catch. Then he saw a fallen tree. He sat down on it. "Want to have my hand steady," he said, addressing the air around him.

The minute Freddie sat down, Cap shoved his long head between Freddie's knees. And then and there Freddie knew that in spite of all the chloroform in the world, he couldn't pull the trigger on Cap. "Pop was right," he said in a sort of wonder. "I just can't do it."

He rumpled Cap's ears, and Cap thumped his heavy tail on the ground. Cap, in spite of his pain, was very happy. He was in the woods again. He was with Freddie.

"There must be some answer to this," said Freddie.

The gun, which Freddie had propped against a sapling, suddenly slipped. As it teetered, Freddie grabbed for it.

FREDDIE didn't come back. His father walked around and around the house, and then presently his mother and father walked around and around the house. Sort of lost like; bewildered like. "The dog's gone too, of course," said Freddie's father. "He might be out by the car now. I mean Freddie."

"Go look," said Freddie's mother. But Freddie wasn't out by the car. Neither was Cap. "I simply don't understand it," Freddie's father said. They had gone back to the kitchen, where Cap always lay. They looked at each other helplessly.

Then there came a whimpering at the back door, then a familiar scratching. Freddie's father whipped the door open. It was Cap all right, but no Freddie. Not till Cap was indoors and under a bright light did they see the raw, bleeding hole in his hindquarters.

Cap lay down and thumped his heavy tail on the floor. Then he got up, moving very, very stiffly, and went over to the back door and nosed it. He stood with his nose to the door till they opened it, then he went out. He began to crawl on his belly.

"He's hurt bad," said Freddie's father. "Hope he leads us to the boy."

Cap did. It was a slow and painful crawl, but he led them all the way. Every once in a while he looked back over his shoulder, to say, "Are you following me?" At the very last,

Cap seemed to make a little run forward. They found him nuzzled tight in against Freddie. His heavy tail wagged, thump, thump, thump.

Then it lifted an inch maybe. Then it lay still.

FREDDIE came awake. He said, "I guess I shot myself in the leg, Dad. I was trying to shoot Cap, but I couldn't. Look, Dad—we can't use chloroform on Cap. It would be cruel. Can't we—can't we find a better way?"

Freddie's father bent over Cap. The big black body had slumped. Cap was dead. He had died happy, doing a job for Freddie. Freddie's father said soberly, "You have my word for it, we'll never chloroform Cap."

"Is—is he all right?"

"Yes, he's all right, Fred. Now let's worry about you."

BEGIN AGAIN

John D. MacDonald

ONE by one and in little groups they all came to see him, the aunts and uncles and cousins and the friends of his mother and father.

Once in a while the kids he had played with came to see him, with a mother along who wouldn't let them get too close to the bed. Of course, all this was after the bad part was over, the hot part where things were all funny and disconnected and you couldn't tell whether it was early or late or even Sunday.

It wasn't hard, really. He had learned to smile politely when they said some of the silly things, and he had learned to thank them for the stuff they brought him. He heard Aunt Harriet in the hall outside his bedroom saying to his mother, ". . . such a shame for an active boy like Robert to be cooped up so long. I bet he's dying to get out there and run around with the kids. And I know how hard it is on you. . . ."

She had walked out of earshot, giving him a chance to think of what she had said. Thinking was a different sort of thing when you were in bed. You could take a thought and sort of hold it up and look at the shape of it, slowly and carefully.

He didn't particularly miss running around. Every day he could hear the yelling when school let out. It didn't hurt to think about it. Every day was long, but not too long, when you learned how to make little things last. The best part of the day was when his father came home from the office.

When the hands of the clock on the little table pointed to four, he began to think about it. He didn't let himself think about it before four. When the thought jumped into his head, he pushed it back down out of sight until after four. From four o'clock on, he thought of something to say to his father. It was always something funny. But, somehow, he never got to say it.

It was always the same. His father would tramp into the bedroom, huge and dark.

"How do you feel today, kid?" he would boom.

Robert would say, "Fine, Dad," wishing his voice wasn't so small.

Then there was the usual joke, when his father said, "Gosh, I sure wish I could spend every day in a nice, soft bed. You got it easy, kid." Then he would laugh and Robert would laugh and, after he had left the room, Robert would hear the distant rustle of the evening paper as his father opened it up in the living room. It was the best part of the day.

At last Dr. Hinkle told his mother that she could prop him up into a sitting position for an hour each day and that he should have something to do with his hands. For a week there were coloring books, clay, and puzzles that had to be fitted together or taken apart. Robert worked on them dutifully, but they weren't satisfying.

One night his father came home with a big board, wax paper, some glass cement, and two boxes of kitchen matches with the heads removed. He laid them proudly on the foot of the bed and boomed, "Know what that stuff is, kid?"

"No, Dad."

"Once, when I was a sick kid, my old man fixed me up with the same layout. Here's what you're to do. You take the matches and the cement and build yourself a big fort on this board. Glue the matches right to the wood. Make buildings inside the fort and when you want windows and stuff, cut them out of the wax paper. Every night I'll inspect the progress of construction and on Sundays I'll help you for an hour. Then, when you're well, we'll take the whole works out in the back yard and be Indians setting fire to the fort. You ought to see one burn! Just like a real one. How do you like that?"

Robert couldn't find the words to tell how much he liked it. The next day, when he could sit up for an hour, his hands shook so with excitement that he couldn't get the matches started properly.

THE next day was better. He found that it was best to set in one match, and then shift to another part, giving the first part a chance to dry.

On Sunday he couldn't do much. Having his father sitting there working with him made his hands tremble again. He was awkward.

At the end of the second week they let him sit up for two hours, one hour on the edge of the bed with a blanket wrapped around his legs. The first time, he felt dizzy and light-headed. The floor looked miles away and the familiar room looked odd from this new angle. Meanwhile the buildings on the big board took shape. He decided on six of them, three on either side of the main street down through the center of the fort. He begged a sharp knife and used it to cut the matches to the exact size he needed.

When the people came about the brace for his leg, four of the houses were done and he had started on the fifth. He was shy about his leg, it looked so awfully thin, like one of the matches, but they didn't seem to notice how thin it was. They made measurements and came back two days later and fitted the brace to the thin leg, telling his mother something about "Merely the problem of getting used to it."

When his father saw the shiny brace of metal and leather and padding, he got a funny tight expression around his nose and mouth, as though he were about to sneeze.

As the buildings in the fort grew, Robert would stop and put his cheek down on the board and shut the higher eye. It was as though he were one of the people who lived inside the fort. The buildings were high above him. In that way he discovered that some of the doors were too big compared with the windows, and he changed them.

One day his mother stood in front of him as he sat on the edge of the bed. He didn't have the blanket wrapped around his legs. She held out her hands and he took them and she pulled him up to his feet. He swayed and would have fallen if it hadn't been for her hands. On the next day he stood a bit longer, and on the third day, with Dr. Hinkle there, he learned how to take a step with the brace on his leg. It was really very simple. It was just a case of stepping off first with the leg which didn't have a brace. Then you lifted your hip so that it pulled the brace off the floor. It would swing by itself, out in front of you, and then you lowered your hip quickly so that the metal ends struck the floor and the brace stayed out in front of you. It hurt to step on it, but not too badly. Not badly at all.

By the first day of spring, the wall around the fort was finished, and with bits of copper wire for hinges Robert was building a gate that would swing. His father had tired of the meticulous work, and while he came in to watch him for a time each Sunday, he didn't help. Each time he would say, "Kid, that's going to burn like mad. We'll have us a time." Each time he said it, Robert felt a small inside contraction as though a big hand was closing around his stomach. But each time he smiled and agreed that it would make a dandy fire.

The first day of spring was also the first day that he could stay dressed all day and walk to any part of the house. He liked walking in on the rugs but not out on the kitchen linoleum. The brace made too much noise on the linoleum. He could almost stop thinking about it when he walked on the rugs.

He used brown watercolor on the matches and it wasn't right. He mixed black with it and it was exactly right. It made the six houses, the wall, the gate, the towers all look as though they were made of logs. He painted the surface of the big board a grass green. With your eyes almost shut, so that everything looked misty, it did look like grass.

His father came home at noon on a warm and sunny Saturday. He smiled down at the fort, rubbed his big hands together, and said, "Kid, it looks like today's the day. We'll have us a fire. I got some color film left and I'll use a portrait lens and we'll sell the pictures to the movies for a million dollars."

This time Robert didn't smile and agree. He opened his mouth and, to his intense surprise, a loud, shrill "No!" came out.

HE glanced up at his father and saw that his father's face had gone all smooth, as it always did when he was annoyed. "What's the matter, kid?"

"I—I don't want to burn it. I want to keep it," he said, dismayed at the sound of tears in his own voice.

His father turned to the door and said quietly, "Certainly, Robert. It's yours. Do anything you want."

Robert stood alone in the room, looking down at the fort. He brushed slowly at the houses with his hand, hearing the crackling noise as he swept them into jagged piles of discolored matches. He noticed that most of the matches were unbroken, that it was the glue which had parted, and suddenly he knew that he had to build again—not a fort but a great house, tall and strong and beautiful. He knew that when he had completed this house which was growing in his mind, no one in the world could bear to destroy it.

With his teeth clamped down tightly on his lower lip, he began to separate the whole matches from those which had been broken.

CARDS DON'T LIE

B. Virginia Lee

As he guided the team along the rocky roadbed, Uncle Ike mopped his face with a bandanna handkerchief and cursed the hot weather. Oh, well—wouldn't be long now. An hour's ride and they'd be in Markleville.

Down inside the coach a young man with curly red hair was talking to a yellow cat that he carried in a basket.

"Well, Trillium," he was saying, "when do you suppose it's going to happen?"

As if in answer to his question, the stage came to a sudden halt. The young man saw through the window that a masked rider was covering the driver. The door on the other side was yanked open and he looked into the muzzle of another gun. He reached for the air.

"Toss out them mailbags, but first give me yer gun."

"I have no gun," the young man said calmly.

He fastened down the lid of the basket. Then he kicked the three mailbags out of the stage.

"Yer roll next," came thickly from behind the mask.

The young man stepped out. He reached into his pocket and handed the other a wad bound with an elastic band. An oddly twisted smile drew up one corner of his mouth —a fact that was noted by Uncle Ike. It wasn't Uncle Ike's first holdup. Less than two months ago his stage had been robbed on a similar lonely stretch, and again a month before that. Only this one was too damned smooth-working, somehow.

"A fine help you were!" Uncle Ike snorted to his passenger as the riders streaked away in a whirl of dust.

The usual crowd had assembled in Markleville to meet the incoming stage.

"No mail, boys," he said briefly as he climbed off his seat. "I was held up again."

When Uncle Ike had finished his recital of the holdup, all eyes turned suspiciously on the young stranger.

Sandy Terris was busy pushing back into the basket the yellow cat. She kept poking her nose out and sniffing.

"Ye mean to say this feller actually pushed the mailbags out to the bandit—just handed them to him?" Pretty Russell asked incredulously.

"He saved his plaything, I notice," Ed Stowe sneered.

"You forgot I lost my own roll," Sandy reminded him.

"Handed it over mighty easy, I noticed," Uncle Ike put in. "Smiled, too, while he was doin' it."

The crowd pressed closer. The sheriff pushed his way through.

"Come clean," he advised Sandy. "It'll be best."

Sandy put the basket on the ground. "I had no part in the holdup," he declared. "I never saw the bandits before. But I can tell you where they are now—with these!"

He put a hand into his pocket and drew out an unbroken deck of cards.

"We tar and feather guys like you out here," Pretty Russell warned.

"Bring him over to my place," Al Crabbe suggested.

Inside it was almost dark after the sun-baked street. At one side stood the old bar, and in one corner a large iron safe. As many as could crowded into the place; the rest stood in the open doorways.

The sheriff and Sandy sat down at a table; but first Sandy lifted the lid of the basket and released the cat.

She stretched, then strolled leisurely off. Sandy watched her for a moment, and then turned to the cards. Before them all he broke the pack and shuffled it.

In front of the bar stood Ed Stowe, Pretty Russell, and Al Crabbe. The cat rubbed her head against Pretty Russell's leg. Then she jumped up on the bar. She went to Ed Stowe, who stroked her head when she affectionately rubbed her nose against his checkered vest.

Sandy was still shuffling. The cat jumped down, strolled around, and leaped up onto the safe, meowing.

"She's hungry," Sandy said.

The sheriff cut the cards. Sandy took one from the deck.

"The jack of spades!" he cried.

He drew out another card. "The king of diamonds!" he exclaimed, pushing away the rest of the deck. "There you are, gentlemen," he said, rising. "Those are the men who did the holdup."

Somebody laughed.

"Say—what is this?" the sheriff demanded angrily, getting to his feet.

"One of the bandits is tall, not over thirty, has black hair and eyes, and carries a gun with an ivory butt. The other looks like the king of diamonds. He is older, stouter, and has hair something like mine. They brought the loot right here to Markleville and gave it to a third man who is acting as their fence. He's hiding it."

THERE was a sharp intake of breath. Nobody spoke, but the way the crowd turned, as a man, in the direction of the three men by the bar showed that they all somehow connected Pretty Russell with the jack of spades and Ed Stowe with the king of diamonds. His red hair fairly shouted guilt.

"The mail and money are right here in this room!" Sandy announced. "Cards don't lie. Some of the money is in the cash register, the mailbags are in the safe—and some more of the money is in that man's vest!" He pointed an accusing finger at Ed Stowe. "Grab those men," he yelled, "if you want your mail!"

Before Russell and Stowe and Crabbe could move they were fanning the air with their hands. Sandy went quietly over to the safe and picked up Trillium. "Back into the basket for you, old girl," he whispered.

"Say," said the sheriff, after part of the stolen loot was found on the three men and the till and safe revealed still more, "who are you and how did you figure that out?"

Sandy turned back the lapel of his coat and displayed the badge of a United States postal inspector.

"Smell that money of mine, sheriff, that you got off the men; take a whiff of the mailbags. They're soaked in *Nepeta cataria*—that's super-catnip. Cats love it!"

ATHLETE'S HEART

Ernest Lehman

LOOK. I know my worry birds. I've been covering basketball games at the Garden for so many years I can spot an aspirin eater from the press box merely by closing my eyes and listening to him dribble. So take my word for it when I tell you that Danny Blake was a worry bird—great out on the court, but even greater in bed, with a thermometer stuck in his kisser, the smell of medicine in the air, and a stethoscope probing at his chest for signs of you-name-it-he's-got-it. Why, I've seen Danny wearing rubbers when the sun was shining, and once I caught him taking his own pulse while I was interviewing him. You get what I mean? Superb set-shot artist, cannonball passer, and an inspired play-maker—but a worry bird.

When he sweated, he worried about catching cold. When he caught cold, he worried about pneumonia. When he ate, he worried about indigestion. When he went to bed at night, he worried about not sleeping. He worried about his weight, torn ligaments, sprained ankles, broken legs, bursitis, tonsillitis, and athlete's heart.

When he made all-American in his second year and all of us called him the greatest player ever to wear the buff-and-blue, he worried that people might think he had a swelled head.

I guess that Harry Kelcey was the only coach in the country who could have handled Danny Blake as well as he did. Kelcey not only knew his basketball, he knew his Danny too, and he loved him as though he were the kid's father.

He wasn't, of course. Danny had a father. Old Man Blake ran a little candy store out in Brooklyn and had such an easy time of it trying to squeeze a living out of life that he didn't need Danny's help around the store more than twelve hours a day, unless Ma Blake's legs gave out and she had to knock off before midnight.

Maybe that's how Danny got to be a worry bird: he grew up in a household that didn't know what security meant, in a neighborhood where a gang of strong-arms lurked around every corner waiting for thin little guys to come along. He never stopped fighting off the phantoms even after an athletic scholarship had landed him in college and out on the Garden

floor against the country's finest quintets and into the headlines as one of the greats of the sports world.

I suppose it was inevitable that sooner or later, he would
get around to worrying about the gamblers. That part didn't
surprise me. What did amaze me was that they had let him
alone. After all, they were trying to get to most of the other
stars in town, and Danny was not only a star, he was the
whole team. What's more, he was a poor boy from a beaten
little family that had only a vague idea of what a buck looked
like.

A beautiful fat setup for the men with the big cigars and
the dirty folding money who enjoyed the thrill of betting on a
sure thing.

Harry Kelcey used to tell me how it was getting the kid
down. Danny was no dope, he knew what was going on.
Danny knew when he was really breaking into the clear and
getting away from the man who was guarding him, and when
it was just too easy to be on the level. He also knew about
the hundreds of thousands of dollars in bets that changed
hands at those college basketball games.

He heard all the rumors about the kids who suddenly
sported new convertibles or whose families moved into fine
homes after a lifetime in a poor neighborhood.

And what he also knew was that the wisenheimers in the
galleries were watching him closely for a sign of the dumperoo.
If any other player racked up fifteen points in a game, it was
fine shooting, but when Danny Blake had an off night, or
the opposition assigned two men to leech him, or he had a
headache, real or imaginary, and he didn't bag something
like twenty-five or thirty, or when the team dropped a close
one, you could hear the nasty cries piercing the cigar
smoke that hung over the arena. No wonder the kid couldn't
sleep nights.

Now, about the game I'm getting around to—I don't know
just how ill Danny really was. All I know is that I saw him
in practice the day before and he appeared to be in good
shape. The sports writers were giving him a careful once-
over that afternoon because they knew that whatever chance
the underdog New York team had of stopping unbeaten Kentucky State and getting a bid to the tournament rested
squarely on Danny's fragile shoulders.

I WAS sitting in the hotel lobby with Harry Kelcey just before
dinner, the evening of the game, when the coach was paged

to the telephone, and I knew from the way his face turned pale that he feared the worst had happened. I walked with him to the phone at the desk and listened to him arguing with Danny in a frightened voice. But it was no go. The kid was home in bed with 103. It had come on him like that. He didn't know whether it was grippe in the stomach or ptomaine or the first signs of polio or what. But he knew that he was far too sick to get out on a basketball court and work himself into a sweat trying to get leaden arms and legs to function, and he was heartbroken, because he knew what it would mean to the team, but what could he do?

Kelcey hung up and his eyes had a beaten, worn-out look. I was sorry for him. They don't come any finer in the sports world. And I was angry at everything in life that makes worry birds out of sweet kids like Danny Blake. But I didn't put any of that in the paper. I guess I'm a lousy sports writer. When I wrote my story on the game after the final horn sounded, I left all that out, and I didn't even hint at what happened afterward.

Danny was lying in bed in his darkened room a couple of hours before game time when his kid brother Marvin came in to tell him that someone wanted him on the phone. Danny didn't want to answer. He said it was either Kelcey, wanting to argue with him, or someone who couldn't get tickets for the game and thought he might have an extra. He told Marvin to hang up and then he turned over and buried his aching head in the pillow, but the kid came back from the phone and reported that the man said it was important. So Danny climbed out of bed, his legs weak and his head spinning, and he went to the phone.

"What do you want?" he demanded.

"This Danny Blake?" It was a man's voice, deep and unpleasant, like a sour foghorn.

"Yes," Danny said. "Who is this?"

"Does the name Rocco mean anything to you?"

"No," Danny snapped. "What do you want?" Just standing up made him feel nauseous.

"Nothing important. It's just that me and a few of my friends are kind of hoping Kentucky shades the locals tonight and we thought that maybe———"

"You thought maybe what?" Danny shouted.

"Take it easy, kid, nothing to get excited about," the foghorn insinuated softly. "I know five hundred dollars isn't *all* the money in the world."

"What five hundred dollars?"

Little Marvin watched his brother with frightened eyes.

"Five hundred dollars," the man replied, "is how much I'll pay for a box of your old man's cigars if you suddenly get so sick you can't show up for the game tonight."

Danny gripped the phone as though he would crumple it in his wiry hands. "Shut up," he said hoarsely.

The man's voice hardened. "Don't be a damned fool, Blake. What are *you* getting out of it but athlete's heart?"

"Cut it."

"You don't have to dump it the hard way. You just don't show, that's all, and the cash will be at the store by game time. Five hundred fish. Remember, it don't grow on——"

"Shut up!" Danny screamed. "Shut up, damn you!" His heart was pounding and his stomach was churning and he wanted to tear this man apart who was filling his ears with vile poison.

"You want to think it over a few minutes? I'll call back."

"Damn you!" Danny cried. He flung the receiver back in its cradle and stood there shaking with helpless rage, his breath coming in little sobs.

"Anything wrong, Danny?" Marvin stared at him.

"Get out of my way." Danny brushed past him and went to the bedroom. The boy followed and stood in the doorway watching him.

"I'll call Ma," Marvin said anxiously.

Danny was pulling a sweater on over the shirt and looking under the bed for his shoes.

"Something's wrong," Marvin said. "I'm going down to get Ma."

"You do and I'll break your neck," Danny snapped as he hurried to the hall closet. The weak feeling in his stomach and legs was giving way to a powerful desire to commit violence on somebody or something.

My story in the morning paper was lousy journalism because it left all this out. It didn't describe the look of astonishment, not to say gratitude and relief, on the face of Harry Kelcey when Danny Blake came running into the locker room about fifteen minutes before game time and started ripping off his clothes to get into the old buff-and-blue.

All I wrote about was the details of the game—how Danny went wild and threw everything but the officials into the basket to score forty-eight points, and how the locals upset

Kentucky State, seventy to sixty-nine. It was one of those thrillers that had everyone in the Garden screaming with excitement, and if you were there you probably heard me screaming too, like a sour foghorn.

LUNCHEON ALFRESCO

J. I. Lawrence

"I AM hungry," said the personage. It was a condescension, a gracious confidence. The captain of waiters beamed, enchanted, and bowed to forty-five degrees. The waiter at his elbow, one pace to the rear, bowed gravely to seventy degrees with the slightest genuflection.

"A dry martini, sir?" breathed the captain.

"Do I look like cocktails? I'm sorry," said the personage, who had luxuriant hair and a Vandyke beard, and clothes of the negative elegance that stamps one as distinguished or wealthy and eccentric. "Just sherry, if you don't mind. You have a good dry oloroso. Cotuits—a dozen. Steady! Don't say cocktail sauce. Mignonette pepper and crushed coriander in a bit of white wine with a dash of tarragon."

"The guinea hen *chasseur* is a menu special for today, sir."

"Specials are doubtful at best. But guinea chicken, yes. Filet *suprême* with *ceps Bordelais*. Salad? Chiffonade—*à la maison* will do—but add half an avocado. Then—a pint of Chablis, slightly cool."

The waiter scurried, the captain subsided. The personage glanced across the low clipped hedge atop the stone balustrade which separated the terrace table from the sidewalk.

"God!" he exclaimed stormily. "What an outrage! Tantalus in Tartarus! Are you hungry, old chap?"

"I use' ter be 'fore it got worse 'n that, sir," croaked the one who stared from outside in.

"Horrible! You know, I'd ask you in, but—your clothes, your—oh, you know! This is a civilized place—a Christian place—and they'd throw you out. You wouldn't mind if I handed you something? Do you care for guinea chicken *chasseur?*"

"Do folks still have ham san'wiches—or—oh, beans is all okay with me, sir."

"Forgive me! You want food. Let me see—er—'Ready dishes.' Here's *ragoût d'agneau à la bonne femme*. That's plain Irish stew with spuds and trimmings. Wait there—I'll slip you the platter. Waiter!"

The captain beat the waiter to the table but paled at the situation.

"But—the gentleman will understand—I am sorry——"

"Don't be sorry about anything! I will do all the being sorry. Just rush the ragout in here before the man dies."

The ragout came, three paces behind the Cotuits, and was passed over the hedge by the personage.

"What! Another one?" he cried. "Your mother, old chap? No? She looks sick. My poor, dear woman, can you take —solid food?"

"An' how, mister! Sure, a ham bone'd be a delicacy if me teeth wa'nt all gone entirely. But, bless ye, I c'd swaller a slice o' ham whole, teeth or no teeth, darlin'!"

"Waiter, two portions Virginia ham and eggs, Southern style—and French pancakes with jelly. Coffee, too, for both of them."

"I am sorry," protested a new voice; "but you know, of course, sir, that——"

"I knew, but scarcely realized that—look at those faces! It makes you feel like a worm, or a monster, doesn't it? But who are you?"

"I am the manager, and——"

"Ah, yes, the manager! And you have your problems, your duty! You'd be glad to invite all the hungry ones in-side, but it simply isn't done. Look there, across the street— a man taking it all in—a reporter, by his looks. The pub-licity will be scandalous. Where did that child come from? He wasn't there before! Starving! Malnutrition and every-thing! What is it you want, child? Milk? Eggs? Meat and potatoes?"

"I'scream cone!" said the big-eyed small boy.

"French ice cream, waiter!" ordered the lord bountiful. "Three portions—vanilla, strawberry, chocolate—meringue glacé, and some macaroons. Hurry up the ham and eggs and pancakes. The poor soul is dying on her feet."

"Look here!" cried the manager. "My dear sir, I can't——"

"Run and catch that newspaperman," counseled the per-sonage. "Slip him three two-bit cigars and tell him you have fed a starving person in all the years you've been a manager. Tell him I'm a crazy poet—or a big oil man from Texas; that's better. There ought to be a cameraman to get a pic-ture."

"The guinea filet and the Chablis, sir," murmured the stunned waiter. "Here, sir, or out there?"

"Here! Fripperies for the satiated, substantials for the perishing! Rush the ham and eggs."

AN interval—a quarter hour of inarticulate murmuring, gasping, smacking of chops—then the personage sighed and got up.

"A policeman is standing at the corner," he informed the captain and the waiter. "You'd better call him before he gets away. The luncheon was excellent. I regret that I have no money."

Blanched faces—swiftly incarnadined, empurpled by reaction.

"Sixteen dollars!" intoned the captain, facing toward the apoplectic manager. "And eighty-five cents!" he added, *largo rallentando.*

"The police!" shrilled the manager.

"Aw, keep yer shirts on!" jeered the old woman over the hedge, and flashed from her bosom a roll of bank notes that matched her wrist in diameter. "Sure, it's meself that'll stake the gintleman! It's a soft heart he has, an' a soft head, too, God love 'im!"

"And you"—frothed the manager—"you took all that food—having all that money!"

"Sure, an' wasn't I invited? What's the likes o' me to be givin th' back o' me hand to a gintleman like him?"

The personage tapped the manager on the shoulder ominously.

"If the beauty of the episode escapes you," he said, "assume at least the grace of silence."

A MAN WHO HAD NO EYES

MacKinlay Kantor

A BEGGAR was coming from the avenue just as Mr. Parsons emerged from his hotel. He was a blind beggar, carrying the traditional battered cane, and thumping his way before him with the cautious, half-furtive effort of the sightless. He was a shaggy, thick-necked fellow; his coat was greasy about the lapels and pockets, and his hand splayed over the cane's crook with a futile sort of clinging. He wore a black pouch slung over his shoulder. Apparently he had something to sell.

The air was rich with spring; sun was warm and yellowed on the asphalt. Mr. Parsons, standing there in front of his hotel and noting the *clack-clack* approach of the sightless man, felt a sudden and foolish sort of pity for all blind creatures.

And, thought Mr. Parsons, he was very glad to be alive. A few years ago he had been little more than a skilled laborer; now he was successful, respected, admired. Insurance. And he had done it alone, unaided, struggling beneath handicaps. And he was still young. The blue air of spring, fresh from its memories of windy pools and lush shrubbery, could thrill him with eagerness.

He took a step forward just as the tap-tapping blind man passed him by. Quickly the shabby fellow turned.

"Listen, guv'nor. Just a minute of your time."

Mr. Parsons said, "It's late. I have an appointment. Do you want me to give you something?"

"I ain't no beggar, guv'nor. You bet I ain't. I got a handy little article here"—he fumbled until he could press a small object into Mr. Parsons' hand—"that I sell. ~~One buck.~~ A dollar. Best cigarette lighter made."

Mr. Parsons stood there, somewhat annoyed and embarrassed. He was a handsome figure with his immaculate gray suit and gray hat and malacca stick. Of course the man with the cigarette lighters could not see him. . . . "But I don't smoke," he said.

"Listen. I bet you know plenty people who smoke. Nice little present," wheedled the man. "And, mister, you wouldn't mind helping a poor guy out?" He clung to Mr. Parsons' sleeve.

MR. PARSONS sighed and felt in his vest pocket. He brought out two half-~~dollars~~ and pressed them into the man's hand. "Certainly. ~~Sure.~~ I'll help you out. As you say, I can give it to someone. Maybe the elevator boy would——" He hesitated, not wishing to be boorish and inquisitive, even with a blind peddler. "Have you lost your sight entirely?"

The shabby man pocketed the two half-~~dollars.~~ "Fourteen years, guv'nor." Then he added with an ~~insane~~ sort of pride: "Westbury, sir. I was one of 'em."

"Westbury," repeated Mr. Parsons. "Ah, yes. The chemical explosion. The papers haven't mentioned it for years.

But at the time it was supposed to be one of the greatest disasters in——"

"They've all forgot about it." The fellow shifted his feet wearily. "I tell you, guv'nor, a man who was in it don't forget about it. Last thing I ever saw was C shop going up in one grand smudge, and that damn gas pouring in at all the busted windows."

Mr. Parsons coughed. But the blind peddler was caught up with the train of his one dramatic reminiscence. And, also, he was thinking that there might be more half-dollars in Mr. Parsons' pocket.

"Just think about it, guv'nor. There was a hundred and eight people killed, about two hundred injured, and over fifty of them lost their eyes. Blind as bats——" He groped forward until his dirty hand rested against Mr. Parsons' coat. "I tell you, sir, there wasn't nothing worse than that in the war. If I had lost my eyes in the war, okay. I would have been well took care of. But I was just a workman, working for what was in it. And I got it. You're damn right I got it, while the capitalists were making their dough! They was insured, don't worry about that. They——"

"Insured," repeated his listener. "Yes. That's what I sell——"

"You want to know how I lost my eyes?" cried the man. "Well, here it is!" His words fell with the bitter and studied drama of a story often told, and told for money. "I was there in C shop, last of all the folks rushing out. Out in the air there was a chance, even with buildings exploding right and left. A lot of guys made it safe out the door and got away. And just when I was about there, crawling along between those big vats, a guy behind me grabs my leg. He says, 'Let me past, you——!' Maybe he was nuts. I dunno. I try to forgive him in my heart, guv'nor. But he was bigger than me. He hauls me back and climbs right over me! Tramples me into the dirt. And he gets out, and I lie there with all that poison gas pouring down on all sides of me and flame and stuff——" He swallowed—a studied sob— and stood dumbly expectant. He could imagine the next words: *Tough luck, my man. Damned tough. Now, I want to*—— "That's the story, guv'nor."

The spring wind shrilled past them, damp and quivering.

"Not quite," said Mr. Parsons.

The blind peddler shivered crazily. "Not quite? What do you mean, you——?"

"The story is true," Mr. Parsons said, "except that it was the other way around."

"Other way around?" He croaked unamiably. "Say, guv'-nor——"

"I was in C shop," said Mr. Parsons. "It was the other way around. You were the fellow who hauled back on me and climbed over me. You were bigger than I was, Markwardt." The blind man stood for a long time swallowing hoarsely. He gulped: "Parsons. By God. By God! I thought you——" And then he screamed fiendishly: "Yes. Maybe so. Maybe so. But I'm blind! I'm blind, and you've been standing here letting me spout to you, and laughing at me every minute! I'm blind!"

People in the street turned to stare at him.

"You got away, but I'm blind! Do you hear? I'm——"

"Well," said Mr. Parsons, "don't make such a row about it, Markwardt. So am I."

CRYBABY

John McClain

IT was almost midnight before they got around to giving the Oscars to the really well-known personalities. A series of guest stars had awarded the prizes to the best scenic designer, to the best special-effects man, for the best technical invention for motion pictures during the year, and to all the other people, so anonymous outside the industry, so important within it.

Now they were giving out the prize for the best short subject, and tension was beginning to mount. The man from the Academy of Motion Picture Arts and Sciences handed the sealed envelope to the well-known director who had been called up to announce the winner. The paper crackled in the microphone as he tore it open. He paused deliberately for several minutes, teasing the audience, then announced the result. There was hearty applause as the winner started for the stage to accept his statuette.

I looked around the theater, recognizing most of the important faces in the business, but not caring much. You see, I was plenty nervous. Myra Caldwell, whom I had brought to the proceedings, was sitting there beside me, and right across the aisle was Joan Weyland. Now, to get the picture properly, you have to remember that during that particular year Myra had played the sensational supporting role in *The Devil Loses* and had been acclaimed practically the greatest find in the history of pictures. But that was the same year that Joan Weyland had stolen a big picture called *Calumet Center* right out from under the nose of one of the most terrific female stars in the industry. The only other actress nominated was not given much chance with the smart money. Now in a few minutes, they were going to announce who had won the Oscar for the Best Supporting Actress of the Year. It was the hottest contest since, the big race in *Ben Hur,* and everybody knew it. Furthermore, it was no secret that the two leading contestants would have been delighted to boil each other in oil—win, lose, or draw. And here they were across the aisle from each other. Do you get why I was nervous?

They were giving out the writers' awards, and I was mopping my forehead frequently with a damp handkerchief, when Myra turned to me and said, in a voice that carried farther than the Consolidated Network:

"Look at Joan. Isn't she ugly tonight?"

I tried to shush her, but it was no good. Several rows of people had heard her and there was a stifled titter. Joan looked across the aisle and glared. Apparently she hadn't caught the words, but she knew they weren't exactly flattering.

Then the lights went down. They were going to run short excerpts from the pictures for which the actors and actresses had been nominated. The supporting-actress pictures were coming on, and here was Joan Weyland in her big scene from *Calumet Center*. The audience started to applaud as soon as they saw her.

After that they ran a short scene from *Whirlwind*, featuring the other nominee, a refugee actress called Tanya Braden. I had never seen the picture or the actress, and the picture hadn't made much money—but, boy, there was no doubt she could act! She played the star's mother and she made you believe it.

Then they ran Myra's big moment in *The Devil Loses*. After it was over I tried to figure who got the biggest hand, but it sounded to me, in my weakened condition, like a dead heat.

"I think I won," Myra said to me.

The lights went up. The elderly actor who had won the Supporting Actor award the year before came through the curtains and prepared to make the award. I didn't see how I was going to live through the next few minutes. He got the envelope from the auditor and very slowly tore it open. He was loving every second of it, the old ham. Then he looked at the little piece of paper.

"The winner," he said, then paused again, "is Miss Tanya Braden, for her performance in *Whirlwind.*"

WELL, I'm not too sure about the sequence of events that followed. I don't remember the applause, because Joan let out a screech from across the aisle that drowned out everything else. Then Myra started to cry. I don't mean cry like the ordinary person, but I mean cry so that the mezzanine shook.

Then Joan got up and started out, and her mother went with her. But I couldn't do anything with Myra. The show was stopped cold and the whole theater was looking at her. I picked her up and carried her out.

It wasn't a very pleasant performance, all in all, but I think there is some excuse. After all, Joan is eight years old, and Myra is only six, and she isn't used to being up so late. I'm a little on her side anyway. And why not? I'm her father.

UP JUMPED THE DEVIL

- Guy Gilpatric

ON the morning of July 4, 1854, the good citizens of New York turned out to celebrate the seventy-eighth anniversary of the nation's independence and an event of even greater local importance.

All through the winter they had heard the thudding clamor of shipwrights' mallets. Early in the spring three masts reared up above Webb's sheds, the tallest of them towering a dizzy hundred feet and crossed by a main yard spanning ninety. Drays came bumping over the cobbles and splashing through the mud of Pine Street, delivering bolt after bolt of new-spun canvas to the lofts—fourteen thousand running yards of it, people said.

After the launching (Mrs. Horatio Seymour, the Governor's wife, had cried, "March down to the waters, brave ship;

I christen thee *Columbia!*") came weeks when the riggers crawled aloft like spiders. And toward the end of June the great ship was towed around to Pier Nineteen at the foot of Wall Street to load a cargo of tools, blasting powder, and chemicals for the California gold mines.

What a clipper she was! Captain John Bannerman, arriving from Baltimore to take command of her, swaggered up and down the wharf in his suit of Shantung silk and his Panama hat of weave so fine that he could drag it through his signet ring, and pronounced her the finest craft afloat.

"Gentlemen," he declared to all within earshot, "I was never one to boast, but if I can't jam this beauty round the Horn to Frisco in eighty days flat, my name's not Bannerman."

"So?" growled a waterside loafer. "And maybe his nickname's not Satan, either! God help the crew that's under him, once he washes off his shore face!"

The *Columbia* was advertised to go out with the tide, eleven A.M., on Independence Day. At a quarter to eleven the city's windows trembled to an eight-gun salute, and a farewell toast was drunk on the quarterdeck.

Now, according to the likeness preserved for us by an old print, Captain Bannerman was a handsome man with a frank, kindly face and a pleasant smile. It is difficult to believe the stories of the change which came over him as soon as he struck blue water; then, it seems, he was invariably transformed into a raging ogre and a fiend incarnate. He had brained one seaman with a heaver, and broken both arms of another. He had kicked a man overboard in a Cape Stiff snow squall for refusing duty when doubled up with ptomaine from rotten grub. He was, said fo'c'sle gossip, Satan himself, from the very instant he completed his usual ceremony of ducking his head into a bucket of salt water "to wash off his shore face" until his vessel reached port. But like most hellship commanders, Satan Bannerman was a reckless sail carrier—a cracker-on who could be depended upon to make quick passages. Thus his services were always in demand by owners with an eye on the profits and none on the brutality which earned them.

At eleven sharp Mr. Wharton, the owner, shook Bannerman's hand, delivered the time-honored formula, "A pleasant voyage, captain, and a safe return," and led the group of visitors ashore. The lines were cast off.

Clear of the Narrows she caught the breeze. Along toward

midafternoon, when with everything set she was reeling off a clean twelve knots down the Jersey coast, Captain Bannerman appeared on the poop.

"Muster all hands aft!" he bawled at the mate. "Stir 'em up, stir 'em up, mister, and shake a leg yourself! This vessel's at sea now, so don't go acting like you're in Trinity Church!" To emphasize his words he thumped savagely upon the rail with the heaver which was slung by a cord to his wrist.

"Come on, you rats, you scum, you mudsuckers!" he shouted. "Gather round down here. I'm going to preach hell-fire to you swine—and give you a red-hot sample of it before you get off this ship. But here—wait—I'll turn this into a testimonial meeting. Hey, Robinson—Robinson, step up here and answer some questions!"

ROBINSON, the Negro steward, was the only man ever known to have made more than one voyage with Captain Bannerman. He had been punished and kicked and beaten into a state of vague imbecility, and seemed to accept abuse as the normal meed of life. He came up the ladder grinning stupidly, and stood beside the captain.

"Now, then," said Bannerman, "speak up, now. Did you ever see me kill a man?"

"Yassuh," said Robinson, shuffling and grinning. "I seen you kill three or fo'. Yassuh, mebbe five."

"What did I kill 'em for?"

"Well, mos'ly fo' bein' slow and sassy, I reckon, suh."

"Yes, that's right." Bannerman turned toward the crew. "I don't stand for laziness and I don't stand for lip. Oh, I guess there was a lot of you curs picked me for a softy when you seen me back there in port, hey? But I guess you've heard about my little trick of washing off my shore face, haven't you?"

He wheeled toward the steward. "Robinson," he barked, "fetch me the bucket of salt water."

"It's all ready fo' you, Cap'n, suh."

"Good!" said Bannerman. "I've learned him his lesson all right. But now, you men, I'm going to stick my face into this brine, and when I take it out you'll see Satan—Satan himself! Watch, now! One—two—three, and up jumps the devil!"

He knelt and plunged his head deep into the wooden bucket. Then, with a howl, he sprang to his feet.

And they did see Satan—Satan or—something! But even

more horrible than the sight were the sounds—the screams—
as the acid lye ate away Captain Bannerman's flesh—and
the shrill cracked laughter of the Negro steward Robinson.

WILMER JACKSON AND THE LEVITATOR
John Gillick

IN 1977, Wilmer Jackson invented the levitator, a small and
simply constructed device somewhat like a tuning fork, which,
when struck, set up vibrations sympathetic to the vibrations
of the human body. The corresponding vibrations had the
effect of creating, through the suspension of gravity, an air
pocket in which the operator of the device could rest while
the earth spun around beneath him.

Jackson was a young physicist working in a small but
complete laboratory which he had built with his bonus from
World War III. After brief experiments he perfected the use
of his device, so that he was able to travel by remaining
static. Encasing himself in an air bubble which he could
elevate by simple muscular movements, he would remain sus-
pended until the revolution of the earth brought his desired
destination directly beneath him, whereupon he would de-
scend and dissolve the air bubble. He also learned to control
its drift, so that he could travel longitudinally. In May, 1977,
Wilmer Jackson was ready to give his invention to the world.

He wanted all mankind to benefit from his findings. Writ-
ing to the television director who programmed news specials
for one of the major networks, he stated that he had perfected
a cure for the world's most dread disease. The director invited Jackson to his office for an interview. Jackson refused
to explain what his invention was, but finally the director
agreed to have the inventor appear on his next telecast.

When he was introduced, he produced the levitator and
described its construction, use and operation. The an-
nouncer asked if the inventor could demonstrate the use of
the levitator to the audience. Although the studio was a
large one, it afforded scarcely enough room to operate the
levitator. Nevertheless Jackson decided to make the attempt,
and moving to the far wall, he elevated himself in an air
bubble. The opposite wall, moving with the earth's revolution,
reached the air bubble in a split second, and Jackson de-
scended amid the tumultuous applause of the studio audience.
When order was restored, the inventor announced his inten-

tion of going to the roof of the building, levitating, and descending at Le Bourget Field, in Paris, on the fiftieth anniversary of Lindbergh's historic flight. Broadcasting facilities were set up to cover the takeoff, and just before Jackson set out, the program director, remembering the inventor's letter, asked him what disease the device would cure.

"Why, war, of course," replied Wilmer Jackson, and lifted into the night sky.

France at that time was just beginning to settle down after a period of political flux. During the previous year the Soviet, announcing that it was impossible to organize the French temperament, had relinquished the protectorate it had established at the close of World War III. The French voted to return to monarchy, and the surviving Bourbon, who was operating a garage in Galesburg, Illinois, was recalled to the throne.

A transcription of the historic broadcast was channeled to France, and the king, accompanied by a huge crowd, was present when Wilmer Jackson floated to a graceful landing and dissolved the bubble. The king introduced himself and asked about the National League pennant race.

Jackson gave a demonstration of the levitator to the public, and then proceeded on his mission. Within a week he had visited all the great capitals of the world and was back in the United States.

The period that followed was the most amazing in the history of mankind. American railroad and airline lobbies demanded the introduction of legislation to limit and regulate the levitator, but so simple was the device, and so easy to use, that all regulation was worthless. A great many small boys allowed their homes to run away from them. The passport became a useless document, since ports of entry were now largely ignored. Substratosphere airlines found their regular lanes of travel cluttered with floating free riders and soon ceased operations.

This confusion was duplicated in every country, and as the nations struggled to find a solution, there occurred the event that marked the turning point in civilization. Within a span of forty-eight hours, about eighty percent of the population of Russia landed in the United States. Food supply, public services, and the maintaining of law and order came to a standstill. The situation was met by the President of the United States. He was of Slavic ancestry, the first of that strain to occupy the White House, and he addressed the nation on television in Russian.

He said that this sudden invasion could bring nothing but destruction to the visitors as well as the Americans, because no economy could be adjusted swiftly enough to prevent famine; that Americans had nothing that Russians could not have in their own country, and that if Russians did not have these things, the fault lay with the leaders, not with the country. He suggested that on their way home they drop in on their leaders to demand a better way of life.

The Russians took his words literally, and within the next forty-eight hours so many of them landed on the roof of the Kremlin that the structure collapsed, killing all the members of the Politburo except the aging leader, who escaped to an Orthodox monastery in northern Greece, where he remained in seclusion until his death two years later. The people organized an enlightened socialistic state and abolished the veto by substituting "Yes, but" for "No."

The slogan "Remember the Kremlin!" was heard in every capital, and politicians for the first time set out to discover what the people really wanted, and gave it to them. War was impossible, because whole corps of soldiers let the rest of the world, including their officers, go by. International boundaries disappeared, and the United Nations Council became the vital governing body of the world. The representatives of the United Nations tried to find an honest and unselfish solution to the problems facing mankind, and they succeeded. Fear was gone, and distrust, and the goods of the earth were used for the betterment of all the people. Hatred disappeared.

A monument to Wilmer Jackson was dedicated in Dubuque, Iowa, his birthplace. In the cornerstone was a permanent record of his famous broadcast, so that if by some catastrophe the great secret was lost, it could be rediscovered. The inscription on the monument read, "To Wilmer Jackson, who lifted Man above himself."

JEDEDIAH MEETS HIS MASTER

Odgers T. Gurnee

JED BROADWATER was the orneriest human in West Virginia by unanimous consent.

For close to thirty years he'd run a thing called the Travelers' Roost, five miles north and two straight up from the B. and O. main line. The meals weren't much, because Jed no sooner got a wife broken in to cooking than she died or quit him. But he barreled his corn liquor in charred wood and it brought brisk trade; that and the entertainment he always had on tap—not free.

He was on the declining end of the most salubrious get-rich-quick idea that had ever sprouted behind his brushy eyebrows, when the peddler came to Travelers' Roost. It was the declining end only because it was too good to last forever. He'd run out of customers.

But the peddler wouldn't know about that, and the old heads around the charred-wood keg could see the minute he drove up and hitched that he was fair game, and the odds were nine to two that Jed would take him.

Standing at the steps to the Roost, the two spoke briefly and Jed led the way inside. Without speaking, the peddler picked up a tin cup that held a half pint when brimming full and cradled the keg in the crook of one arm. He drank it neat and he drank half a pint.

"Good likker, Mistuh Broadwater," he said, setting down the cup.

Jed glowered. "Where'd you hear tell my name?"

The lean one wiped his lips. "Oh, round about."

"An' what else would you 'a' been hearin'?" Jed inquired.

"Well, now," mused the peddler, "fer one thing, that you was poison mean."

Jed edged around the counter. "Yeah?" he demanded. Then, "Yeah," spitting into the pine-knot fire. "Poison mean and proud of it." He flung a massive arm east and south. "They ain't nobody grew no meaner but one—my pap."

"An' he's dead," said the peddler.

Jed's arm stopped short. "How come you know that?"

The peddler slipped a lean hand across his eyes. "I was borned with a caul," he whispered. "Hit's a gift."

He turned and ambled out, and somebody on the far side of the keg let go a stifled yawp of laughter. Jed kicked open the sagging door and followed in time to see a giant of a dog rise from beneath the wagon bed. The hackles stood like spikes as Jed approached.

The master of Travelers' Roost stopped short.

"What," he asked bitingly, "is that there thing?"

THE man with the gift winked broadly. "That there's a cross

'twixt sudden death an' a saurodinus. But I got another pup which is some dog."

Jed looked at the bulk beneath the rear axle and shivered. "What kind?"

"Huntin' dog."

"Where's he at?" Jed insisted.

The peddler began to dig under the wagon seat with his back turned. "Right here," he said, swinging around.

In the bend of one elbow he held the most forlorn-looking hound north of the Tennessee line.

Jed's eyes popped. Then he roared with laughter. "Great day!" he shouted. "Half rat and half rabbit." He stopped abruptly. "What," he demanded, "do you reckon he kin hunt?"

"Coons," asserted the peddler solemnly.

"And badgers?" suggested Jed.

"An' badgers," went on the owner.

Jed motioned toward the barn lot. "Come yonder," he urged. "I got me a badger he cain't hunt."

The group in the keg room joined them. They knew about the badger. At a shale bank near the barn Jed halted. A barrel had been sunk into the earth on its side. A screen covered the open end.

"I got fifty says yore houn' cain't get him out," said Jed.

The peddler knelt and eyed the interior. In the dim light he could see the badger's tushes.

"Bet," he said emphatically.

Jed's face clouded. "You wouldn't wish to make it a hunnerd?" he ventured.

The peddler frowned. "I'm sorta outa cash, mistuh," he apologized. "But I got a good hoss and waggin an' I'm packin' four hunnerd in stock," he murmured.

Jed hurried to examine the horse and wagonload. He returned by way of the house, carrying a leather pouch.

"Eight hunnerd," he affirmed.

The peddler stopped and looked into the barrel again. "My pup has got to git him outa there?" he asked.

"To oveh this line," amended Jed, dragging his boot heel across the hard ground two feet from the barrel mouth.

The peddler rose. "Count yore money, big boy."

Jed laid the assorted bills on the ground and straddled the barrel, gripping the wire door.

"When I jerks her up, you lets him go," he counseled.

The peddler took his position with the dog between his knees.

"Git!" he shouted.

The wire shot up and with a swinging motion of his arms the peddler turned the hound and pitched him into the barrel —*tail first.*

Then he planted one huge foot on the money and gripped a broken ax handle in his good right fist.

There was a bellow from Jed, a yelp and a snarl from within the barrel, and the dog came out in sprawling, terror-riven leaps. Fast to his back with tooth and claw came the badger.

As they passed the peddler, he swung his ax handle. It caught the scratching passenger flush between the eyes and knocked him into unconsciousness.

Still in motion, the peddler faced about toward the oncoming Jed, seemed to pick his spot with deliberate intent, and then chopped the hard ash firmly and efficiently into the Broadwater teeth. Jed sat down suddenly, spitting molars and curses.

The peddler scooped up the bills, inspected the quite dead badger, and then returned to his erstwhile antagonist. He pointed at a shattered incisor in his own jaw.

"Recollect seeing anythin' like that afore?" he asked pleasantly.

Jed, who had started to rise, relaxed abruptly, and shook a bruised and befuddled head.

"Which goes to show," the peddler asserted sadly, "what a pore remembery you got."

He bit a large chew off a bright Burley twist.

"You give me that," he said, indicating again the half-portion tooth, "the day you knocked me off'n pap's mule and lit out frum home. I'm yore baby brother Claude an' I'll be right glad to tell the folks you ain't doin' so well."

His foot was on the wagon shaft before any of the spectators recovered the power of speech. "Hey, mister," someone called, "You ain't forgettin' yore dawg?"

The peddler flourished his whip and laughed gaily. "Yo'-all kin keep him fer a sooveneer," he called. "I jist borried him frum the feller down the hill who tole me about this badger business."

SNAKE DANCE

Corey Ford

"HELLO. That you, Mom? . . . Oh, I'm sorry, operator, I thought I was connected with . . . No, I'm trying to get long-distance. . . . What? . . . Centerville, Ohio . . . I told that other operator. . . . What? . . . I *am* holding it."

He fished nervously in his pocket for a pack of cigarettes, pulled one cigarette out of the pack with his thumb and forefinger, and stuck it swiftly between his lips. He glanced at his watch and scowled. The game had been over for a half hour. The snake dance would be coming down the street this way any minute now. With his free hand he tore a match from the paper folder, and propped the telephone receiver for a moment between shoulder and ear while he struck the match on the flap. As he put the match to the tip of the cigarette, a thin voice rasped vaguely inside the receiver, and he whipped out the match.

"Hello. Mom? . . . Oh, I'm sorry," he mumbled. "How much?" He took a handful of silver from his pocket and began to drop the coins into the slot of the pay telephone. He could hear someone speaking above the echoing reverberations inside the phone.

"What? Oh. Mom? Hello, Mom. This is Jerry. I say, this is——Can you hear me now? . . . Sure, I can hear you fine. . . . Sure, I'm all right. I'm fine. And you? . . . That's fine.

"Mom"—and his voice seemed to falter for a fraction of a second. Then: "How is he? Is there any change?"

There was a tiny silence.

"Oh." His voice was a little duller when he spoke again. "I see. Yeah. This afternoon, eh? And that other specialist, he said the same thing? Um-hmmm. . . . Oh, sure, sure. No, of course, Mom, there's nothing to worry about. No, I'm not worried; I only just called to find out if there was any change, that was all. . . . Did they say if he could ever— I mean, can he move his arms any yet?" He gulped. "Well, that doesn't mean anything, really. . . . No, of course, all those things take time. Sure, a year, or maybe even less. . . . What?"

He took a second cigarette out of his pocket and thrust it between his lips nervously. He lit it from the stub of the first one and ground out the stub beneath his heel.

"What money? Oh, you mean I sent you last week? Now, Mom," impatiently, "I told you all about that already in the letter, didn't I? . . . Sure it's a scholarship. I got it for playing football. And so naturally I didn't need all that money you and Pop had been saving up for me to go to college, and so I just thought maybe, with Pop being laid up now for a while and all . . .

"Where? Why, right here." He frowned. "No, this isn't exactly a dormitory; it's—I live here in the fraternity house, you see. Sure I'm in a fraternity. It's the one Pop wanted me to join, too, tell him. . . . No, honest, Mom, it doesn't cost me a cent for my room. It's on account of my football."

He opened the folding door a little. He thought he could hear the band in the distance.

"Who, me? Homesick? Not so you'd notice it." He laughed. "I'm having the time of my life here. Everybody's so swell. I know practically everybody here at Dover already. They even all call me by my first name. Say, if you don't think I'm sitting pretty, you ought to see my fraternity house here." He gazed out through the glass door of the phone booth.

"Every night the fellows sit around and we drink beer and chew the fat till . . . Oh, no. No, Mom. Just beer. Or usually we just go down to Semple's for a milk shake. . . . No, that's only the drugstore. . . . No." He smiled slowly. "I promised you I wouldn't drink, Mom."

In the distance now he could hear the sound of the band approaching.

"Well, Mom, I gotta hang up now. The gang'll be here in a minute. We're having a celebration after the game today. We played Alvord—took 'em sixteen to nothing. . . . Sure I did, the whole game; you oughta seen me in there. I made two touchdowns. Everybody's going down to Semple's after the game, and I gotta be ready, because of course they'll all want me to be there too. Can you hear the band now?"

It was growing louder, and the eager voices in the snake dance could be heard above the brasses, chanting the score of the game in time with the band.

"Now, listen, Mom. One other little thing before they get here. Mom, see, I'm going to be sending you about ten or twelve dollars or so each week from now on until Pop is better. . . . No, Mom. Heck, I got plenty. Sure, they always fix you up with a soft job if you're a good enough player. The alumni do it. . . . Here they are now. Hear them?"

The band had halted outside. Someone led a cheer.

"That's for me, Mom. . . . Sure. Didn't I practically win the game for them today? Hear that?" He kicked open the door of the phone booth.

He held the receiver toward the open door of the phone booth. They were calling, "Jerry!" "Hey, Jerry, hang up on that babe!"

"Hear that, Mom? Now goodbye. And look, by the way, if you should ever happen to see Helen," he added carelessly, "tell her I'm sorry I couldn't ask her up to the freshman dance like I'd planned, but with the football season and my scholarship and all—— Tell her, Mom. She—she didn't answer my last letter. Okay, Mom. Tell Pop everything's okay, see? Now don't worry. . . . Bye."

He replaced the receiver slowly on the hook and stared at the mouthpiece a moment. As he opened the door and stepped out of the booth, he could see his reflection for a moment in the tall mirror behind the soda fountain—the familiar white cap, the white jacket with "Semple's" stitched in red letters on the pocket. The crowd was lined along the soda fountain, shouting, "Jerry!" "Milk shake, Jerry!"

RELEASED FROM CHANCERY

Llewellyn Hughes

IN support of this story [Hardisty began] I am prepared only to say that I believe it was not a product of the young lady's imagination, and I must admit that her telling of it gave me the shivers.

(We were gathered around the club bar, and the conversation had turned to supernatural manifestations. Every instance brought up had been gunpowdered by explanation and ridicule by the storyteller himself. Hardisty, the critic, was the last person thought to take a less cynical view.)

Some years ago [Hardisty began again], when I had a city editor's desk in Raleigh, North Carolina, we had with us on the paper there a girl of haunting beauty, her flaming red hair accentuating the pallor of her oval face and giving to her slate-blue eyes an unforgettable sorcery.

Possessed of a quick and keen mentality, she was active on the tennis court, in the swimming pool, and, apart from her unusual appearance, was the average up-to-date young American girl.

Her name was Mary Howard, and she claimed descent from William de Warenne, first Earl of Surrey.

This first Earl of Surrey had, for his services in the Norman Conquest of England, been given the honor of an estate in what is now known as Yorkshire. William Howard, Mary's late father, had spent most of his money in an unsuccessful effort to claim this property.

The estate, an old Tudor mansion built on the ruins of a Norman castle, was in chancery; or, as we have it over here, in equity. That is, the Court of Chancery refused to give a clear title to the claimants. There could be found no documentary proof of marriage between William Howard's great-grandmother and great-grandfather, the latter being the last rightful heir.

This was the situation at the time I knew Mary Howard. I may say, without impairment to the story, that she has now fully established her claim to the estate, and is living there, in Yorkshire, as Lady Armond, wife of a wealthy English baronet of that name.

Now, the history of the eighteenth-century marriage questioned by the Court of Chancery is vague and brief. It was the time of the Jacobite disorders, and by some unknown hand the husband was murdered. His bride soon followed him to the grave, surviving just long enough to give birth to a son.

Now, I want you to bear in mind the fact that William Howard of North Carolina, unable to afford a trip to England in connection with his claims, had been forced to conduct his negotiations from this side of the Atlantic.

Neither he, his wife, nor his daughter—an only child, by the way—knew what the old Tudor mansion looked like, since photographs of it were unavailable.

But the Howards were in possession of the reproduction, in color, of a portrait of their great-grandmother—a great work of art, it was, painted by Gainsborough.

I saw that reproduction myself, and to my astonishment Mary Howard was the living image of the lady in color of hair, salient eyes, oval face, pallor of skin, even to the tapering fingers of her exceptionally beautiful hands. No question of direct ancestry there!

MOST probably born out of her father's long struggle to

gain possession of the property, Mary constantly dreamed of an old castle.

Finally, years after the claim had been abandoned as hopeless and William Howard was no longer alive to pursue it, Mary won a trip to England, and, once there, decided to go to Yorkshire and visit the old family estate.

Partly crumbled to ruin, its rectangular windows and its gables broken and fallen away, it was being dismally looked after by an old withered caretaker who managed to eke out an existence in its moldy interior.

"To my absolute amazement and dismay," Mary Howard told me on her return, "it was the castle of my dreams! The Jacobean doorway, framed with classic forms, starkly presented itself to me in fact. The fantastic chimney treatment I recognized at once.

"The old caretaker kept staring at me, his mouth drooling, not saying a word. When I asked permission to go inside, he seemed to shrink away from me.

"Everything I saw in the interior I was quite familiar with, through my dreams. The staircase, which I had convinced myself could only have been a figment of my subconscious brain, was actually there before my eyes: a staircase divided into short flights, at right angles to each other, around a central open well. I had walked up and down them a hundred times in my dreams.

"The chimney piece I knew well. Before its frieze and cornice of Tudor design, its rich paneling above, I had often stood vainly trying to warm my chilled hands.

"It held me in a trance. But the shock of it was as nothing to what followed. On a sudden feverish thought, I turned to the caretaker, who seemed stricken with palsy.

"Is this old mansion haunted?" I inquired fearfully.

"His aged eyes took on a terrified expression and his trembling lips barely moved.

" 'Yes, madam,' he said, crossing himself. 'It is haunted by you.' "

AUNT MINNIE AND THE ACCESSORY AFTER THE FACT

Samuel Hopkins Adams

It was the most open-and-shut case in my police experience. We had everything—corpse, motive, murderer, and a man on the spot at the time. And what was the result? A complete washout.

You remember the West Sixteenth tenement murder last fall, the one the newspapers headlined as the MILLIONAIRE BEGGAR MYSTERY. I figured on being in those headlines myself. DETECTIVE CASEY LANE SOLVES MILLIONAIRE BEGGAR MYSTERY. And look at me now! I might as well give my badge to Aunt Minnie.

Old Hans Gommer wasn't any millionaire. But he'd made enough out of forty years' street begging to own the tenement. He kept it up decently, too; otherwise Marian and I wouldn't be living there. His room was at the stairhead, second floor, same floor as our apartment. It was a single room. And I mean single; not even a toilet; just a stove, a bed, a stand, a couple of chairs, and a few cooking gadgets. The windows were barred with fixed half-inch iron, five inches apart. The old miser was jittery about being robbed. His door was like a bank vault's.

He hadn't a friend in the world, unless you count a big snarly brindled tomcat that used to crawl the narrow ledge along the wall, squeeze through the bars, and beg for what was left of dinner, and little enough of that, I guess. Old Hans had a relative, though, an ugly little wizened devil of fifty or sixty—you couldn't tell—who used to come in two or three times a week for an unfriendly game of backgammon. His name was Finney, and we found out afterward he was a disbarred lawyer from somewhere out West. When the door was open in summer, you could hear the pair of 'em growling and cursing and swapping charges of crooked play. True, too, I wouldn't wonder.

The door wasn't open this Monday evening. It was cold and rainy. My wife had been busy all day organizing a floor-by-floor bond campaign with a barrier across the foot of the stairs so no tenant could get past without buying. She and Ma Sanderson were on guard from five o'clock on. At half past, old Gommer went out and came back with a flounder tied up in paper to cook for his dinner, and Marian sold him a twenty-five-cent stamp. That was his limit. An hour later Peter Finney, the nephew, knocked on the door and was let in earlier than he usually came, though if he expected to get a meal out of it, he was a fool.

Maybe they quarreled over that. Maybe over the game. Anyway, Finney stabbed Hans expertly through the spinal cord, and what happened in the next three hours the police department is still arguing. All but me.

Don't forget that all this time either my wife or Ma Sanderson, or both, were on the barrier looking right up to old Gommer's door. Even a cockroach couldn't have got in or out without being spotted.

It was half past nine and I was smoking my pipe and jollying with the two females at the foot of the stairs when Finney showed up above us.

"Uncle Hans is dead," he said. He was white but cool enough.

The door hadn't sprung shut. We all ran up and went in. The old boy was dead all right, with a neat hole in the back of his neck, so small you could hardly see it through the fuzz of gray hair. He was in his chair, half slumped over the table. The checkers and dice were scattered over the floor. I put it to Finney.

"Who did it?"

"I don't know."

"Why don't you know? You've been here all the time."

You never saw a fishier eye than the one he gave me. "I was asleep," he said.

I turned to the two women. "Could anyone else have got in here since this man came?"

"No." Both spoke at once.

"Could anyone have got out?"

"Absolutely not," Ma Sanderson answered. But my wife qualified with, "Unless those window bars are movable."

I tried them. They were solid.

"I guess that puts it up to you," I told Finney. "Where's the knife?"

"I don't know."

Well, I ought to have called headquarters, but I figured that, being Johnny-on-the-spot, here was my chance of glory.

"I saw old Gommer having one of these narrow-bladed little fish knives ground by a street grinder one day," Ma Sanderson put in.

"That's it," I said. "We'll find it."

First I frisked Finney. He hadn't so much as a penknife on him. Then the three of us fine-tooth-combed the room. Not a sticker of any sort. That left the window as the only answer. Fifteen feet opposite was a blank wall. Far as it could be thrown, the knife would have to drop into the little back yard. I gave Marian my gun to guard Finney and went down with my flash. No knife. And no footprints in the soft ground, proving that nobody had happened by and picked up the knife.

"It's *got* to be in this room," I said.

So I went through Finney again and the three of us turned the place inside out and made a detailed inventory of everything in it. It was then that my wife said:

"I wish Aunt Minnie was here."

Aunt Minnie was her old schoolmarm at No. 18, now living on the top floor of our tenement. But she was on a visit.

"You can have Aunt Minnie," I said. "I'll take headquarters." So I phoned.

Then I went after Finney again.

"You killed him."

"I did not. What would I want to kill him for?"

"You're his heir, aren't you?" Marian said.

"I guess so. But I didn't kill him."

"Now, listen," I said. "You got into a stink over your game of backgammon and maybe he made a crack about you cheating and you let him have it. If you didn't, who did?"

"That's for you to find out," he said.

Then the headquarters push came in and did everything over again with the same result. They took Finney with them when they quit, leaving us with only one new fact: the old man had probably been dead about three hours. So he must have been killed shortly after Finney arrived—which got us a lot nearer nothing.

"I *do* wish Aunt Minnie was here," my wife said.

"What would she do that we haven't?" I growled. I was getting sore. The headquarters bunch acted like they thought I'd botched the thing somewhere.

"Aunt Minnie'd find something we've overlooked," Marian said. "There was never a trick played in school but what she caught the funny boy that did it."

"Anyway," I said, "we've got the guy, if we haven't got the knife. It's a watertight case for the D. A.'s office."

THE district attorney didn't see it in that light. "Find me the knife," he said, "and I'll put him in the chair. But you can't convict a man of murder because nobody else did it."

"That's what Aunt Minnie says," said my wife when I told her the case was at a standstill a week later. "I had a letter from her. She'll be back next week."

When the old dame arrived, she had us up in her room and listened to Marian and Ma Sanderson and me.

"Where's Finney?" she asked.

"Out of jail. He got a lawyer who sprung him."

"Have you got that inventory you made?"

I handed her a copy. She studied it. "Is this everything that was in the room at the time?"

"I'll swear to that," Marian said.

"So will I," said Ma.

"You spoke of the old man bringing in a fish in a parcel."

"That's right."

"Where's the fish?" she asked.

"He ate it, I suppose."

"Did he eat the bones? I don't see 'em here."

Marian and Ma and I looked at the inventory.

"You've got the wrapper down: 'Square of brown paper.' Where's the string?"

"Oh, to hell with the string!" I said. "Are you figuring that he wound up the knife in the string and swallowed it?"

"I never did like comedy cops," Aunt Minnie said. "Not even in the movies. If I were after that knife, I'd look on the roof."

"What roof?"

"This roof and any other roof contiguous."

"Look, Aunt Minnie," I said. "Babe Ruth himself couldn't reach out between those bars and flip a knife five stories up onto a roof."

"You'd better do as Aunt Minnie says," my wife told me.

There's a lot of rubbish on tenement roofs, but I found the knife, two buildings away back of a chimney. Anyway, I found *a* knife and a fish knife at that. Of course there wasn't a chance of fingerprints after it had been out in all that weather. I brought it back to Aunt Minnie.

"Find anything else?"

"I wasn't looking for anything else."

"No fishbones? No string? No brains!" said Aunt Minnie.

So I went back and brought in the lot. "Who put 'em there and why?" I asked.

"In the jargon of your district attorney, the accessory after the fact."

"Oh, yeah? And how did he get 'em?"

"Why, I suppose the murderer passed 'em out through the window."

"Easy, like that! And how did he reach the window? Jump up eighteen feet from the courtyard and hang to the bars? Or scrounge his way across that ledge?"

"Funnier than ever," said Aunt Minnie, "but not too smart. The ledge."

"How could any man navigate a six-inch ledge?" Marian wanted to know.

"He couldn't. A cat could. Many's the time I've watched that ugly tom make it on his way to old Gommer's window."

"Wait a minute!" I said. "Are you telling us that a tom-cat would carry away a knife and hide it on a roof?"

"If it was fixed up right, he would."

Then I began to get it, but I didn't like it. "How am I going to put that up to the D. A.?" I asked. "The department's in wrong enough already on this case without any accessory tomcats."

"I wouldn't," she advised. "I'd leave the D. A. out of it."

"So the murderer not only gets out but collects his legacy, does he? That kind of gripes me, Aunt Minnie."

"Well, I wouldn't be so sure of his collecting," Aunt Minnie said. "You didn't know that I once taught drawing, did you?"

She wouldn't explain that crack until Peter Finney's death. He had received a large envelope in his morning mail and collapsed in the hallway when he opened it. On recovering, he went to the drugstore for medicine, but bought rat poison instead. Beside his bed they found a little of ash where he had burned that piece of mail.

Aunt Minnie looked pretty solemn when she got the news. "Perhaps it's just as well," she said, "though I didn't fore-see quite that result of my experiment."

"What was in your letter, Aunt Minnie?" my wife asked.

"It wasn't a letter. It was a freehand sketch of a cat crawling on a ledge with a fish bound around with string in his mouth, and a knife handle sticking out beyond the fish."

Which goes to prove, my wife says, that women know more than men about a lot of things, including logic and cats.

Maybe so.

IN CHARACTER
Richard Connell

At midnight I had to go back to the studio lot to get some notes I'd forgotten. That day it had swarmed with a thousand extras in vivid Spanish costumes. Now it was a ghost town, naked and soundless in the moonlight.

From the shadows of one of the vast, hangarlike sound stages a man came shuffling. He moved slowly, feebly, an old man, incredibly whiskery and shabby. His clothes did not fit him, nor did his skin. He carried a large pan of milk.

I said, "Good evening."

He returned my greeting in a voice like a rusty echo. "Workin' sorta late, ain't you?" he remarked.

"Yes. Rush job," I replied.

"They all are," he said, and his grin showed a few stumpy teeth.

He set the pan down and emitted a sibilant sound, half whistle, half hiss. From a dozen dark corners loped alley cats of every hue and age.

"Movie studios are fulla rats nowadays," he explained. "So I got this job—casting director for a mess of cats. I laid off two last week. They wasn't the type."

He favored me with that wide wry grin.

"If I owned all this," he said, and the wave of his hand took in the studio and the surrounding Hollywood, "I'd let the rats have it."

I said, "What's the matter—don't you like movies?"

"Sure," he answered. "Only they don't make 'em no more." He sighed.

"I seen 'em come and I seen 'em go," he said. "Well, I warned the big brains in the front office what would happen. I told 'em, 'Who wants to set in a theater and listen to gab, gab, gab? You don't expect pictures in museums to talk, do you?' I said. 'Pictures are pictures,' I said. 'Go on and let 'em gab,' I said, 'and, mark my words, in a few years the audiences'll have earaches and you'll have headaches. You're killin' an art,' I said. They put the sneer on to me."

He pushed aside one sated cat to make room for a hungry newcomer.

"And now look!" he went on. "There's hams around this very lot beatin' bum gags into a mike and draggin' down five thousand fish a week that couldn't of played stooge to one of the old Keystone Cops back thirty or so years ago when acting—I mean *real* acting—meant something. Remember Tubby Kling?"

"Tubby Kling?" I groped. "Let me see now—wasn't he——"

"An ace comic," he said. "But the Johnny-come-latelies never heard of him. Tubby Kling didn't need no high-priced writer to make him funny. Tubby *was* funny. Nowadays they sweat and stew for months on a script, but Tubby never needed no script. They'd just say to him, 'Tubby, you're a cuckoo that's just escaped from a nut house, see, and you think you're a jelly roll, see? So you hide in a bakery, and when the cops come you do your stuff with the cakes and things.' In one day Tubby would turn out a laugh routine that would have 'em rollin' in the aisles. That was actin'. Now you take this opera they're makin' on this lot—what do you call it?"

"Latin Love," I told him.

"Don't make no difference whether it's Latin, Greek, Chinese, or Eskimo—it's all a lotta mouse meat," he declared. "They been fussin' and finaglin' on it four months already, and I'll bet a million it won't have one half the belly laughs Tubby Kling used to get in a two-reeler he knocked out in a week."

I said *Latin Love* was not meant to be funny.

"It will be," he said. "Though not on purpose. Gab, gab, gab! Some doll-faced goof blattin', 'Won't you sit down? I wonder!' Why, Tubby Kling could do more with a look and a wink than them tramps can do with a dictionary. You've seen that fancy ballroom set on Stage Three, ain't you?"

"Yes."

"Cost about forty thousand smackers," he said. "Well, when Tubby Kling made *Pie à la Mud* it cost only ten grand—and half of that was his salary. All the props he had was a fright wig, a wagonload of pastry, and a dozen cops—and they're still laughin'. That's actin', son."

"I'd like to hear some more about the old silent days," I said. "Let's go across the street to Packy's place and have a bite to eat and maybe a drink."

"Much obliged," he said. "But I can't leave my troupe."

He grinned round at the cats.

"Besides," he said, "I don't feel any too chipper tonight. Pain in my pump."

"Sorry to hear that," I said. "Well, good night."

The detaining hand he laid on my arm was like a fall leaf.

"Want to do an old-timer a favor?" he said.

"What?"

"I could use a pie," he said.

"I'll bring one back," I said. "What kind?"

"Any kind will do," he said; and added, "Coconut custard, if they got one."

I brought him back his pie. He thanked me and shuffled off into the gloom.

When I came into my office at the studio next morning, my secretary said:

"Here's your mail; and there's a story conference on *Latin Love* at eleven; and there was a bit of excitement round here this morning—"

"What?" I asked.

"They found an old fellow lying in the ballroom set. Heart failure, I guess. Funny angle on it, too. From the looks of things, he'd been smacked in the face with a custard pie. Nobody seems to know much about him—his name was King or Kling or something like that."

THE BRIGHT EYES OF DANGER

Donald Barr Chidsey

KERRICK knew that dinner on the train would not be good, so he went across to the Majestic. His heavy Gladstone bag he left behind, but he carried with him a small square metal case and kept it next to him. Even without his big Sikh, Kerrick felt reasonably safe. But it was odd about Bhan Singh.

When he returned, his Gladstone had been moved into a sleeper. He followed it and the train started.

After a while he yawned and went out into the corridor, carrying the case. He saw no porter or guard. The other compartments seemed empty. Kerrick leaned against the flimsy iron gate of the rear platform and watched the track skitter away. The jungle had been cleared for twenty-five or thirty yards on each side of the track, but it pressed close in the darkness.

Kerrick went back to his compartment, closed the door behind him, snapped on the light, and then said, "Oh!"

The man wore plain white drill and a large white topee. He sat riding backward. His legs were crossed, and on the upper knee rested a small automatic pistol. The muzzle faced Kerrick.

"My name is Thorne. In case you're interested. Turn your back, please, while I pat you." He removed the revolver from Kerrick's pocket. "Now then, sit down. Lock the door first, and leave that case here."

Kerrick obeyed. Then he lighted a cigarette.

"Don't you think this is all pretty wild?"

"Not necessarily. I'm not even on this train, as far as anybody knows. I came up second-class, and when they attached this sleeping car I slipped in and hid under a seat."

"What do you want?" demanded Kerrick.

Thorne smiled. "You work for the American jewelry firm of Spitz Brothers, and a certain Siamese prince in that firm's office in San Francisco recently picked out twenty enormous uncut grass-greens. He left orders how he wanted them cut. You're delivering them now."

Nervousness jerked at the corners of the man's mouth. His eyes flicked to Kerrick's case.

"I'd estimate they are worth twenty thousand pounds."

"The price his Highness is paying," Kerrick said suavely.

"You've been jolly careful to keep this case by you. In Singapore you even hired a Sikh bodyguard."

"What happened to him, by the way?"

"I didn't do it," Thorne shrugged. "Merely arranged for it."

The train rocked back and forth.

"Do you plan to steal my case and jump off?" inquired Kerrick, smoking. "You'd be in a pretty wild neighborhood."

"No, I'm not planning to do that."

"The porter will come soon to make up the berth."

"But when he comes *you* won't be here. My topee is just about the same as yours, and so is my suit. I'll have your ticket and passport. When we get into Penang, I'll go to the Runnymede for breakfast, carrying the case. I'll leave the bag. Before the train starts again I'll be at sea in a fishing *prau*. Day after tomorrow I'll be back in Singapore."

Kerrick said slowly: "And me?"

"You," said Thorne, "I shall shoot. Afterward I'll toss

your body off the back platform. No train is scheduled to pass here for two days. A bodyguard will undoubtedly be waiting for you at the border, but your bag will still be here, and they'll assume from the porter's story that you missed the train in Penang."

Thorne needed to talk, to justify himself to himself.

"The pleasantest part is that before any investigation can get under way I shall be on a P. and O. ship headed back for home. Departing by request. I've been warned I'm to be declared an undesirable British subject. Alleged to have been consorting with Asiatics and that sort of thing."

"Opium?"

Thorne shrugged. "I'm not going back a poor man, I can tell you!" He looked at his watch. "In three and a half minutes we'll whistle for a small native village. And if you've ever heard this whistle you'll know that a pistol shot couldn't possibly compete with it."

With his left hand he patted the small metal case.

"Toss me the key; I want to look at those emeralds."

Using his left hand, watching Kerrick all the while, the Englishman put the case flat on the seat by his side. He inserted the key Kerrick handed him, and turned it.

"You be careful," he warned, lifting the automatic a little from his knee. "The safety catch is off."

Thorne threw back the lid of the case.

What he saw caused him to scream in high fright, springing to his feet, stumbling toward the window.

Kerrick bounded out of his seat. Thorne swung the automatic toward him, and fired point-blank into Kerrick's belly. But before Thorne could fire again Kerrick had his right wrist and was forcing it high.

Thorne fell back. Kerrick humped his shoulder twice, very hard, into Thorne's face, so that Thorne's head was banged against the wall. The automatic clattered to the floor. Thorne slid into a heap.

The whistle was blowing.

A SIAMESE officer met Kerrick at the border. "Your baggage, of course, will not be examined." He nodded at the metal case. "And that is for his Highness?"

"It is, but it's not what you think. Another man made that mistake, and he's in jail in Penang now." Kerrick opened the case. "I had heard that his Highness was interested in these, and I brought one as a personal gift."

"Ah!" The officer's dark eyes shone. "A beauty! The biggest *kongrang nuoc* I've ever seen!"

He lifted the brilliant green snake from the case, handling it like a connoisseur. He knew it was non-poisonous.

"I kept it with me all the while," said Kerrick. "I didn't want it tossed around and possibly getting bruised. The emeralds," he added, slipping a curved metal case from under his shirt, "I kept even closer to me. The stones are all right, but the case got a bit nicked." There was a groove on its outer surface. "I shall keep it, though. It's been very good to me."

RICH MAN

Everett Rhodes Castle

GRANDFATHER was a philosopher, and like a lot of philosophers, I guess, he was a mild-mannered man who was always ready to admit that there are two sides to every question. So when people got to arguing with him, or around him, about things that they got heated up and il-logical about, like politics and religion, he would tell this story that Doc Eaton told him one day up on the Hill.

It happened a long time ago, when the town wasn't all steel and concrete and automobiles; when you could still hear the whir of a lawn mower without taking a streetcar out to the suburbs, and still see a horse lazily switching at the flies on his flanks under almost any sycamore tree. The Forest City had a lot of trees in those days.

And it had a lot of people that didn't always see eye to eye, like a lot of other cities. And it had a rich man, like almost every other town. And this rich man was a pillar in the Baptist Church; and people didn't see eye to eye about him, either.

There were those—and Grandfather's eyes twinkled when he said it—that claimed the rich man was an old hypo-crite, that he was ruthless in his business dealings, that he was so tightfisted he wouldn't spend a nickel to see an earthquake, that when he went to church on Sunday morn-ing he was almost as important as God to a lot of people.

Then there was the other school of thought. It asserted that just because a man had made money under condi-tions as they existed was no reason to call him a lot of hard names. In fact, they asserted stoutly, the people that called him names were merely envious of his success. They maintained he went to church not because he was a sanctimonious old fraud but because he was at heart, and for all his money, a simple, deeply religious man.

It was while these two groups were hot at it that the rich man gave a party. Well, it wasn't exactly a party, Grandfather would explain. It was more like a shower for the pastor of the church. One group of parishioners saw in their invitation nothing but a kindly, neighborly gesture. The other just said it showed how miserly the old buzzard was—getting other people to do what he could have done a thousand times over without feeling it a mite.

Grandfather said even then he had the sneaking feeling that the rich man wasn't so insulated and isolated by his money that he didn't know what people were saying about him, and that that was the real reason he gave the party.

But both sides of the question went to the party. A lot of them were pretty curious about the inside of a rich man's home.

They brought offerings for the pastor, as they were requested. Some people brought apples, and others brought sides of bacon and onions and other homey old-fashioned things like that. But nobody was really much interested in what the other guests brought. They were all waiting for one thing. What would the rich man bring out? Even Doc Eaton, the preacher, according to Grandfather, couldn't help wondering about what was coming. You could feel the undercurrent of suspense.

And then the rich man brought out his offering.

It was a bushel of potatoes. They were nice potatoes, extra large and scrubbed white and clean. But still and all, they were only a bushel of potatoes that anybody could buy in the Old Market for a lot less than a dollar.

Well, sir, Grandfather chuckled, you could practically see what people were thinking. They were the people who were saying to themselves and to everybody else, "Well, what did I tell you?" And then there were those who made it perfectly plain that they thought it was mighty tactful of their host not to make an ostentatious parade of his money before a lot of neighbors and friends.

But the host went around as if he didn't notice anything, though Grandfather always insisted that he detected a little twinkle in the rich man's eyes as he shook hands with all his fellow parishioners and wished them good night.

The preacher toted his gifts into his house, and just because they had been the center of interest, so to speak, he picked one of the big white potatoes out of the basket. Then he noticed that one end of the potato had been opened. He investigated, and discovered that a silver dollar had been neatly inserted through the opening. He examined every potato in that bushel basket, and there was a silver dollar in every single one of them.

At this point Grandfather usually sat back and plucked benignly at his white beard and smiled. Then he'd turn philosopher and say:

"It takes an almighty pile of gall for a man to sit up and say what is going on in another man's mind, don't it? I mean one way or another. When Doc Eaton told me that story he didn't bother to point out any moral. By the way, he don't do any preaching any more. He's been a congressman from New Jersey for years and years. But I guess the story has a moral, all right. Always sort of tickled me, like it must have tickled Doc's rich parishioner.

"The New Testament says it is easier for a camel to go through the eye of a needle than for a rich man to enter the kingdom of God. Well, I ain't saying it isn't true. But I am saying this: It took John D. Rockefeller to put a silver dollar through the eye of a potato in order that a lot of people could have some food for thought."

NO HOLDS BARRED

F. R. Buckley

THIS was when we were sailing from Tutuila to Tonga after French Pete had knifed the Kanaka. We didn't know about the knifing, or Captain Swenson wouldn't have given Pete passage; he was all seaman, Swenson, and probably the best schooner sailor in the South Seas, but he did have a respect for laws. Harbor regulations and the law of storms, alike, the captain was all for them. However, since Pete had his passage money and nobody had found the Kanaka's body yet, of course the question of law didn't arise, and we sailed on schedule with that angel in our midst. We weren't twenty-four hours out before he brought up the subject of poker, nor thirty-six before he'd got a game going with me and the captain, the third mate, and a trader we happened to be carrying. Pete lost twelve dollars.

"I like it, even when I lose," says he. "It's a man's game, poker. Anything you can get away with is yours, and no right and wrong. Only you're bound to give a man his revenge when he wants it. Don't forget that, Captain, will you?"

"You play a cutthroat game, all right," says the trader. "I suppose you really know that four cards don't make a flush?"

"They do if you can get away with it," says Pete, grinning more than ever. "By the way, there's something *you* can remember, mister. Nobody but the party calling has a right to remark on the showdown. It's man to man, and if the caller can't tell a spade from a club, that's up to him."

"Seems a funny spirit to put into cards," says old Swenson in his mild way.

"This isn't cards," says French Pete, getting up. "It's poker. Good night."

Well, you might have thought that talk would have warned us, but it didn't. For one thing, Swenson and me and the first mate were getting all the warnings we could use from the barometer. There was dirty weather somewhere around; we didn't have any wireless, and for all his nose for storms Swenson couldn't just figure where this was. He was worried; which is probably why he drank the next night. Had one in French Pete's cabin before dinner—and he wasn't a drinking man—and by the time we sat down to give French Pete his revenge, he seemed all kind of dazed. I have a suspicion that Pete may accidentally have dropped cigar ash into that whiskey and soda.

"Cert'nly we'll play," says the old man, when I hinted the game might be postponed. " 'S law of the game, like Leblanc says; must give a man his revenge when he wants it. Stick to the law an' you'll never go wrong. I wish this damn' storm would. Whose deal is it?"

"Mine," says French Pete; and it was, and his game as well; he certainly got away with murder. The captain lost nearly four hundred dollars.

He came on deck next forenoon kind of shaky. Pete was standing with me near the taffrail.

"Too bad about last night, Captain," says he.

Old Swenson looked at him. "You owe me a revenge, I think?"

"Any time you want it," says French Pete. "Only don't imagine just staying sober'll make you a sure winner, Cap.

I play one game under last night's conditions, and another under others."

"You've got a swell idea of cards," says I, disgusted.

"We weren't playing cards," says Pete, starting for'ard. "That was poker."

Swenson didn't say anything. Nor did I. We fixed our position, worried some more over the barometer, and didn't play poker that night.

It was three days later when Swenson—he'd been studying about that storm all afternoon, and powwowing with the third mate—said at noontime that maybe he'd take his revenge that evening.

"Anything you can get away with is yours," says French Pete. "But I wouldn't be too sure, Captain."

It was at eight bells that we found our storm, or the tail of it; and by nine that night we were getting a fair dusting. Swenson wouldn't have a Kanaka at the wheel; he had the third mate there, and the second on watch, which left four of us for the game. The trader and me had figured this fight would be strictly between Pete and the old man; we weren't going in much.

"It's almost too rough——" began Pete; and as he said it the *Susie* did what I'd never known her to do—gave a cavort that nearly threw me out of my chair and banged Pete's head pretty painfully against the bulkhead. Moreover, it seemed from his color that he might be feeling the least bit seasick. I looked at Swenson, but he took no notice. He was just finished shuffling the cards when *Susie* gave another roll that sent the whole deck flying, and made French Pete turn from yellow to pale green.

Well, Pete may have been a brave guy when it came to knife work and such, but certainly he had no taste for salt water. Though I'm free to admit that at times *Susie's* antics made even me cock an eye at the old man, wondering whether we hadn't both better go on deck and take a look-see. He didn't allow suggestions from his officers, and since he wouldn't catch my eye, nothing happened about it. Except to Pete; and what happened to him was aplenty. By four bells Pete was the color of shoal water and wanted to quit; but the old man wasn't taking any. He said this was the revenge Pete was bound by his own law to give him; there'd be no other chance to play, and the game was going on.

AND how! Talk about poetic justice! Swenson didn't pull any stuff as crude as Pete's that other night, but he bluffed like a madman, and Pete simply didn't have the stomach left to take chances. So he lost steadily: first the four hundred he'd won; then another hundred; and then he was positively through. His head was rolling on his shoulders, and he hadn't the strength to hold his cards.

" 'Sides," he gasped, "no—more money."

Swenson laid down his hand.

"All right," says he calmly; and then to me: "Being we're all square now, mister, you might as well go tell the third mate to put her on her course again and stop this steeple-chasing before we snap the sticks out of her. Gosh, he had me scared once or twice when he jibed her. Tell the mate to reef down and give her some foresail."

I'd been kind of suspicious for some time; but it was a brand-new idea to Pete. I saw his eyes sort of widen.

"You—you mean—you've been having—ship act this way—on purpose?"

Swenson looked at him and smiled.

"You see," says he, "this isn't cards. It's poker!"

EASY MONEY

George S. Brooks

"You may ask," said the plaintiff's lawyer. He nodded to Lee Gould.

The attorney for the State Line and Southern Railroad got up wearily, glancing at the penciled notes he had made on the back of a company envelope. He was licked before he began this cross-examination. The woman would get every dollar she asked for. The jury was with her.

He looked at her appraisingly for a moment before he fired his first question. It was hard to upset a woman's story, because women were never afraid of being prosecuted for lying.

She flushed a little under his steady gaze.

"Mrs. Rogers," he began suavely, "I'm not going to question you about the railroad accident in which you claim to have received certain alleged injuries. We admit that such an accident occurred at the time and place and substantially in the manner described here. In fact the railroad did offer you, and still offers you, a substantial sum of money to salve those injuries. After consulting your attorney you refused that golden salve. Is that correct?"

"Yes, sir."

"Upon the advice of your attorney, you came to trial in the hope of recovering greater money damages?"

"Yes, sir."

"You ask us for twenty thousand dollars?"

"That's right."

"Speak a little louder, so we can all hear you. Did your attorney tell you this was easy money?"

"No."

"You were in the hospital, in bed, in a private room. Your attorney was admitted. Did he tell you this was easy money?"

"I don't remember." She flushed.

"Why didn't you mention this back injury when you were first admitted to the hospital, following the accident?"

"I did."

"I have here, Mrs. Rogers, a sworn record of the injuries you claim to have sustained. On this record I find that you did not tell the surgeon about a back injury until after you had conferred with your attorney, twenty-four hours after the accident. Why was that?"

"I don't know."

Lee Gould smiled. "Did your attorney tell you, after he had sent the nurse from the room, that a back injury was the one type of injury we could not disprove by medical testimony and X-ray pictures?"

"No." She flared up angrily.

"Did he tell you that when a patient refused to sit up, and groaned if the nurses moved her——"

"He did not tell me to groan."

"Ah. You thought of that yourself," said Gould. "Today, a full year after the accident, you are still wearing a surgical corset to support your back?"

"I am."

"You testified under oath that you would not be able to sit in that witness chair without your corset?"

"I am not able to sit erect without it."

"You heard your own surgeon admit on cross-examination that if a normal uninjured person was strapped up in a surgical corset such as you are wearing for twelve months, the normal person would be unable to sit erect without support."

"Something like that." Her eyes snapped.

"That's all, Mrs. Rogers."

But he knew it was no use. Three jurymen had "Soak the railroad" plainly written on their faces, while four others were thinking, "Poor little woman!"

"Easy money," he told them, when he summed up. "Damages against a railroad are easy money. Easy for this plaintiff to ask. Easy for you to award. But, gentlemen, in times like these, beware of easy money!"

The judge's charge was fair and brief. The jury retired. In forty minutes they returned. "We find for the plaintiff in the sum of twenty thousand dollars."

Swinging his briefcase, Gould hurried down the street. He'd get the devil at the office. Twenty thousand dollars and costs! More than he could earn in two long years.

Eight o'clock already. No time for a decent dinner with his wife. He'd have to grab a bite at a counter and go up to the office. He was due in court at nine thirty tomorrow morning for the Reynolds suit, and it wasn't even put together yet.

He wondered why he'd let himself be sidetracked on these liability cases. If he could only afford to get away from it for a few months, build up a decent practice of his own!

THE railroad terminal building was deserted when he entered the lobby. He rang for the elevator.

The car came down, but it shot past the ground floor. Through the grille work and ground glass, Gould saw the old watchman tugging at the control switch. But the car did not stop. With a sickening crash that shivered glass three floors above, the cage hit the bottom of the pit.

"What a dandy action against the building!" was Gould's first thought. "That old elevator was condemned twenty years ago."

He ran down the fire stairs to the subcellar. Twisted and crushed like a pasteboard box lay the wreckage. He felt the watchman's wrist. No pulse. Dead.

The lawyer wiped his forehead. "What an escape!" he thought. "I might have been in the elevator." Then another idea made him pause. Twenty thousand dollars. Two years' pay. Easy money. He smiled. "On second thought, I *was* in the elevator."

He crawled into the telescoped cage, squirmed under a twisted girder, lay on his back, closed his eyes.

"Oh! Don't touch me. Don't! My back. My back!" he cried, when the rescue party tried to move him.

OFF SIDE

Howard Breslin

CURT WHEELER, the sports editor in the guest box, touched his host on the arm. "Neat," he said. "They get to work like the pros."

The broad-faced man nodded. He was more responsible than anyone else for the fact that the home team was out there at all.

The visitors punted. The safety man took the punt on the run, pivoted, and cut between the ends. One missed him cleanly; the other dived and was brushed aside. He came back twenty yards before he was finally forced out of bounds.

"Who is that?" asked Wheeler.

"Tug Morton," said his host. "The fullback."

Morton picked up seven yards on an off-tackle smash. The man who made the tackle didn't get up. Morton walked away without even glancing at him.

The visitors called time. When the referee called the teams back into position, they lined up noisily, calling insults across to their opponents. The home team came out of its huddle with the silent speed of military discipline.

Morton didn't carry the ball, but two men broke through and threw themselves at him anyway. He kept his feet.

Wheeler whistled. "They're going to work on Morton. Won't your boys get sore?"

"They won't fight back. It's forbidden. Any dirty play and there'd be no more football at this institution."

The home team hammered its way toward the goal line. Whenever Morton carried, the opposition piled on. Even after a penalty. Morton always got up; sometimes enemy players didn't.

Finally the big fullback, picking a hole in the line, shot through and went eight yards for the game's first score.

From the home stands an "Ah-h-h!" welled up, then stopped as if cut short.

After that the visitors wilted before the pounding

of the home eleven. Two more touchdowns were added
to the score. Morton figured in the last with a long pass.
He had a strange face, high-cheeked and heavy. Only the eyes,
quick beneath thick brows, showed any expression.

In the third quarter Morton plucked a pass from an end's
fingers. He was off along the sideline. It happened too fast
for his mates to give him much blocking, and nearly everyone on the other team had a clean shot at him. Most of
them never laid a finger on him; three bounced off his churning legs.

"Touchdown!" said Wheeler, hammering on the arm of
his seat. "That boy stops for nothing!"

"That's why he's here," said his host.

The referee called it off side. A group of players gathered
around him, arguing. The official waved his arms.

Morton made no attempt to argue with the decision. He
took his place and stood quietly. But his hands were clenched
into fists.

The visitors shifted into a short-punt formation. Morton
pranced forward; he signaled a halfback to change position.
The half went back to safety. Morton crouched behind his
own line.

With the snap of the ball, Morton went through the
scrimmage line as if it weren't there. He smashed a blocking
back into the kicker. All three crashed down together, but
Morton scrambled up and dived for the bounding ball. One
of the visitors was there ahead of him, and the impact
sounded like a shot. Morton came up with the ball.

Wheeler, cheering, turned toward his companion. But
the man was staring at the field, a worried look on his
face. "I was afraid of that," he muttered.

All three of the players who had come into contact with
the charging Morton were lying flat. One got to hands
and knees, then toppled over. Morton, ignoring them, was
waving his teammates into formation for the next play. He
stamped with irritation when the whistle shrilled for time.

"See, Curt. The off side robbed him of a touchdown. He
wants that back. And everything in his way goes down
until he gets it!"

Wheeler shrugged. "What's wrong with that? It's in the
game!"

"It isn't a game with Morton."

"But—that's what makes him a great competitor. A money

player. With the old killer instinct. Dempsey had it. Grange——" He stopped.

The other nodded. "It's what makes him a great athlete, maybe. It's also what brought him here! Five years ago he was engaged to a girl. She fell for some other fellow. They both went to tell Morton. He felt he was being robbed of something that was his. He went berserk. He struck and killed that lad his girl fell in love with."

"Then he's in for——"

"Life," said the warden.

"Ah-h-h!" Another scream went up from the crowd of convicts as Morton raced over the goal line with the prison team's fourth touchdown. Morton, for the first time, was showing his teeth in a smile.

THE GREEN MOUSTACHE

Frank Bonham

THERE are a hundred canyons within a mile of Hangtown. Unfortunately for Stephens, he never reached the first one. The horse played out. Of all the horses in town, he had stolen a spavined one.

The miners dragged him to the jail. One of them threw a carpetbag on the floor. The others, rough men in rough clothes choked with the red dust of the mother lode, held the prisoner. "Noose bait, Sheriff!" one of them said.

Sheriff Hannaford studied the prisoner, a tall man, slender as a lath, with dark hair and pale eyes. "You don't look like a fool," he said. "How'd you come to steal a spavined horse? We don't hang them any higher for stealing a quarter horse than a jackass."

The miners roared.

"An oversight," the thief said. He could still smile.

Hannaford questioned him further and made entries in a daybook. *Name: Finn Stephens.* "Occupation?" he asked.

"Card sharp," said one of the men. "Amateur. Give the devil his due, Sheriff—he didn't have much time to pick and choose over the horse. He was in a hurry."

Hannaford, after locking the man in the end cell, went through the bag. He had a weakness for imagining dramatic backgrounds for the men he dealt with. This one, an Alabaman by his speech, he pictured on a fine white horse—his own—giving his darkies hell for not picking enough cotton.

He saw him tall and graceful in a drawing room or bending over a lady's hand to pay a compliment. These things his parents had taught him. But they had neglected to teach him a trade. So when the crop failed and he lost the plantation——

Hannaford checked himself. Sometimes he thought he ought to have been a storyteller. He was a large, loose-jointed, yellow-moustached man in his middle years, with round silver spectacles. The moustache was patterned after General Custer's. Sometimes he would pose in front of a mirror with his hand tucked in his coat. He knew himself to be bashful and uncertain, but he had achieved a reputation for steadiness and courage.

He came across a flat box full of brushes and twisted tubes. He grunted. An artist! A famous one, no doubt; exiled for taking liberties with the wife of some nobleman whose portrait the artist was painting. He was tempted to ask about it. He refrained. It was harder to hang them when you had become interested in them.

The next day a west wind brought the choking fumes of the smelters into Hangtown. Grimacing at the nauseating taste of sulphur, Sheriff Hannaford carried the prisoner's dinner to his cell. Staring through the grilled window, he saw Finn Stephens hunched on his cot. Stephens was coughing. He arose in agony, gasping for breath.

Hannaford unlocked the door. "You didn't have enough grief havin' TB. You had to steal a horse, too!"

"Not—TB!" Stephens gasped. "Asthma. Damned fumes. Get me—every time."

"Asthma, eh?" Hannaford's ready sympathy leaped up. "Doc Jennings has a cure for asthma. Want I should call him?"

"No cure. But—try anything once."

DR. JENNINGS came in half an hour. The sheriff watched curiously while he sprinkled crystals on a bit of blotting paper in a saucer and touched a match to the paper. He placed it on a stool, told Stephens to kneel before it, and threw a blanket over him. In five minutes Stephens' voice said: "Good Lord, Doctor! What is this? It's remarkable!"

"Saltpeter," said the doctor. "Some European discovered that the fumes are good for asthma. I'll leave some in case you have another attack."

In thirty minutes Finn Stephens was breathing normally.

He turned the crystals with his finger. "Saltpeter!" he said. "Ordinary saltpeter." He regarded the sheriff intently, frowning a little.

Hannaford cleared his throat. "Holler when you're through eating."

Stephens nodded. Then, as Hannaford was going out, he said quickly, "Sheriff!" He stepped close and ran a finger-tip down Hannaford's jaw. "I have never," he said slowly, "seen such a jawline as that. Never."

Hannaford grasped the butt of his gun. "Hold on, mister! I ain't took it in *that* easy!"

Stephens' hand fell away. "I—I'm sorry, Sheriff. Really, it was quite spontaneous. I'm an artist, you see. You have a fine jaw, what I would call a—well, a military jaw."

Self-consciously, Hannaford grinned. "It's a cavalry jaw. You can hang horseshoes on it." He smoothed the General Custer moustaches.

It was unfortunate for Finn Stephens that the circuit judge was in town. In the morning he was arraigned for horse stealing. Hannaford asked him, "You deliberately stole that horse? You weren't drunk?"

"I am afraid I wasn't," Stephens said pleasantly.

He was sentenced to hang on Saturday.

That evening the sheriff was surprised to find an ex-cellent likeness of himself sketched in charcoal on the adobe wall of Stephens' cell. The artist had used charcoal from the sheet-iron stove in the corner. "Like it?" he asked.

"It's right clever," the sheriff conceded.

Stephens regarded it critically. "I have three days. I might be able to do some kind of portrait, if you like."

Suspicion's cool finger touched Hannaford's neck. "Sure," he said. "Only, of course, you'll have to do your studyin' through the bars." And he grinned.

"That's all right. I'll want my paints and some canvas."

Hannaford stroked his moustache. A tug of war began in his mind. It was his official duty to suspect Finn Stephens' generosity. But the dark hollow features were without guile. "All right," he said.

He brought the paintbox. The artist rummaged through it. "Damn! Completely dried out! And there wouldn't be any supplies closer than Sacramento." Then he snapped his fingers. "You've got assayers by the dozen. They'll have minerals I can use for pigments. It may be unorthodox, Sheriff, but we'll have a picture!"

HANNAFORD brought the minerals and a mortar in which to grind them. He had a frame made and stretched heavy duck over it. Stephens mixed his paints and daubed at the canvas. The sheriff's face emerged, moustache first.

Hannaford watched the likeness of himself come to life, the eyes bold, the jawline stark. It was not the man Hangtown knew, but the one who now and then posed before a mirror. The sheriff began to wish that, somehow, he could make it easier for Stephens to go, for go he must.

Yet the artist seemed to have forgotten about it.

"Waiting to swing doesn't seem to bother you like it does most," remarked the sheriff.

Stephens shrugged and put a tiny catch-light in the sheriff's right eye.

The portrait, when it was finished, was better than the picture of the woman behind Finney's bar. The sheriff wished it were someone else he was hanging in the morning. This was a sincere and intelligent man who had lost sight of his star somewhere. . . .

AT three thirty in the morning the dull stroke of an explosion awoke the sheriff. He thought at first it was an untimely shot among the mines. Then he knew it was too close for that. He heard sounds in the corral. There was a strong beat of hoofs in the alley.

Grabbing his trousers, Hannaford ran to the jail. Clouds of smoke churned in Finn Stephens' cell. By the light of the lantern, Hannaford discovered that two of the bars of the window and a section of the mud wall had been blown out.

Some men ran up the street from the saloon. They were too far in their cups to be of much help. "Stephens!" the sheriff shouted. "Someone must have slipped him some black powder! He's blown out half the wall."

This time the artist had taken the best horse in the corral —Hannaford's.

THEY found the horse some weeks later, but they never found the horse thief. Hannaford was secretly relieved. With an election coming up, he didn't want it to get around that the sheriff himself had supplied the powder for Stephens' escape.

It had been several days before he'd figured out that all the materials for black powder had been in Stephens' cell for two days. Saltpeter, charcoal, and sulphur. Sulphur that he himself had brought for yellow pigment. Ground fine in the mortar, tamped day by day into a hole a sharp stick could have drilled in the adobe wall, the powder had unlocked the door.

The sheriff was not an ungenerous man. He held only one thing against the artist. Stephens, just before he left, had impudently tinted the Custer moustache alfalfa green.

A GOOD LITTLE FEATURE

M. C. Blackman

HE was a shabby little old man, but his shabbiness was that of the country worker rather than the city poor. It was obvious that he had never been in a police station before.

"Do you want to make bond?" the desk sergeant asked.

"I dunno," he quavered, and it was plain that he did not understand what a bond was.

"You can put up one hundred dollars cash to guarantee your appearance in court tomorrow morning," the sergeant explained.

"That's a heap of money," the prisoner protested.

"You can telephone someone to come down and make your bond."

"Don't know nobody."

"I'll have to lock you up, then." The sergeant turned to a patrolman. "Search him and take him downstairs."

The prisoner did not like the idea of being searched, and when the officer discovered and removed a cotton bag pinned beneath his shirt, he protested volubly.

"Gimme back that, now. That's mine. You hain't no right to take it. You're a-robbin' me, and I won't stand fer it."

The desk sergeant gasped. "Say, old man, don't you know it's dangerous to carry all that money with you?"

At these words a young man sitting in one corner of the cage threw aside his magazine, arose, and strolled up to the desk.

"How much dough has he got, Sergeant?"

The officer pointed to a pile of bills he had removed

from the cotton bag. "Must be at least five thousand dollars," he estimated.

"It's fifty-five hundred there," the prisoner corrected. "Silas Jones paid me that for my farm when me and Ma decided to move to town. Silas can tell you the same, and I'll thank you to give it back to me."

The police reporter for the Riverton *Evening Star* was interested. He read aloud from the docket: " 'Henry Tucker, Nine-one-six Tenth Street, petty larceny.' What'd he steal, Sergeant?"

"About seventy cents' worth of groceries from that chain store at the corner of Tenth and Cherry streets."

"With all that money in his pockets!" the reporter marveled.

" 'Tain't so!" the prisoner shrilled indignantly. "I warn't tryin' t' get away, like they said. I was lookin' fer the feller in charge of that crazy store. I never stole nothin' in my life."

The reporter laughed. "He's probably telling the truth."

"Listen, old man," said the sergeant. "There's no need for you staying in jail when you have money to make bond." Very carefully and patiently he explained the nature of a bond, and finally the prisoner was made to understand that his one hundred dollars would be returned to him after his case had been heard in court.

"And do I get the rest of my money back now?" the prisoner asked.

"Yes, but you better take it to a bank before somebody robs you."

"I been aimin' to, but me and Ma just got here and I hain't had time t' pick me out a good bank."

The little old man pinned his money under his shirt again and departed. The reporter looked at the clock.

"Almost time for the edition," he said. "Guess I'll drag into the office."

"Wait a minute, Charlie," the sergeant called. He followed the reporter to the door. "I wouldn't print anything about this if I were you."

"Why not? It's a good little feature."

"If you publish that story the old man will be robbed of his life savings before morning."

The reporter hesitated. "Guess you're right, Sergeant," he agreed reluctantly, "but I hate to lay off. I could have made a good funny story out of him. However, I don't want to get the old man robbed."

Nevertheless, the final edition of the *Evening Star* carried the story on the front page under a two-column head. And, as the reporter suggested, it was a good little feature. He had made the most of his material, treating the incident humorously but sympathetically.

"WELL, how'd you like my story, Sergeant?" the reporter asked on the following morning. "Wasn't it a good one?"

"Yes," the officer agreed unsmilingly, "it was a good story. But you promised me you wouldn't use it."

The reporter chuckled. "Well, I haven't seen the morning sheet, but I'll bet a buck our country friend wasn't robbed last night."

"No. He wasn't robbed."

"I thought not." The reporter was well pleased with himself. "You see, I followed the old man out of here, took him to a bank, and saw him deposit his fifty-four hundred. After that——" Something in the officer's face stopped him. "Why, what's wrong, Sergeant?"

"You should have mentioned the bank deposit in your story," the sergeant said in a tired voice. "Henry Tucker was murdered in front of his home last night. We found his bankbook in the gutter."

BEDTIME STORY

Phyllis Duganne

THE gray sky seemed as close to the earth as the canvas top of a circus tent, and the rain fell in a steady, limitless downpour. The headlights of the green sedan cast a thin lemon-colored glow upon the asphalt of the street. Beyond the city limits a traffic signal turned red, and the man at the wheel stopped the car and looked up at the familiar granite wall that he could almost have reached out and touched.

Behind it, the huge prison was a murky shape against the dusk and the rain, and he shivered. The signal flashed green, and the sedan shot swiftly forward and into a side road, rutted and narrow, rising steeply, resembling at the moment a shallow brook. From the peak of the hill a driveway zigzagged to the shore of the lake, which lay like a fallen piece of the wet gray sky before an unlighted frame house.

By the time he had opened the garage doors the man was soaked. He closed them and crossed with quick, springy steps to the house; entered the unlocked door. His wet shoes made a soft sucking sound upon the rug, and as he reached the table, barely visible in the dimness, he stiffened, alert, warned by the trained perceptions of nearly seventy years that someone was in the room.

He struck a match, and above the quick bright flame his eyes met the eyes of a man seated in his armchair; saw the blue steel of a revolver pointed at him.

"Shall I light the lamp?" he inquired.

"Yes."

Visibility flowed from beneath the white china shade over the pleasant room, with rugs and books and bits of polished brass and copper, a chessboard set out on a small table.

"Sit down," said the man with the revolver. "No—not by the door—over here!" He waited grimly. "I want some money and the keys to your car. And keep your hands out of your pockets!" He got up and felt the pockets of the man in the chair.

"Never carry one—anymore," he murmured. His bright quick eyes burned upon the intruder's face, dropped to the revolver. It was his own. "Escaped from the prison?"

"Let's skip the conversation," suggested the young man brusquely. "Give me your car keys." He held out his left hand for keys and wallet, the gun steady in his right. "How much?"

"About twenty dollars. More than they'd give you at the prison if you waited for them to open the door."

"Yeah?" said the boy. "I'm going to trouble you for some dry clothes, too."

His eyes, blue and deep-set, had that look that prisons give.

The old man led the way into his bedroom. "There's the closet. Get kind of tired of gray, don't you? I know—I served thirty years there myself."

The boy stiffened. "If you think you're stalling for time, you can save your breath."

"Is Lennihan still guard on Corridor Twenty-eight?" The boy's eyes flickered. "Which wing were you in? They tell me that new block of cells has all the comforts of home." He chuckled, never taking his eyes from the boy's face. "How'd you make it, anyhow? Just the curiosity of an old man—I can read about it in the papers tomorrow."

"Maybe," said the boy grimly.

"Maybe," agreed the old man. "Think they won't catch up with you? Didn't you ever hear the words, 'You can't win'?"

The boy stood still. "I can win what I'm after—I think," he said. "Were you really—in that place?"

"Thirty years," he repeated calmly. "And here I am now, living where I pass it every day. Human nature——"

"Is pretty rotten," interrupted the boy shortly. "You have no telephone."

"And it's a long walk to the nearest house," added the old man. "You can tie me up." They looked at one another, a measuring, calculating sort of look. "You're a fool, you know," the old man said.

"You're telling me?" The boy's grasp was firm upon the revolver. "Want me to tell you a bedtime story before I leave you? One jailbird to another, huh?" He moved the gun.

The old man sat quietly, waiting.

"All right, I'll tell you who I am. I'm the office boy who has to go to his grandmother's funeral the day the big-league ball game's playing—you know? Only Gramma's really getting buried. I'm the hero of that sob story about the fool who took the rap for somebody else, and then has to break out account of his kid sister's going to marry the skunk. Honest! Only I don't expect you to believe it!"

"I believe it," said the old man.

"Yeah?" said the boy. "I wonder." He laughed. "You asked me if I expected to win. I'm still winning, even if I'm back in jail tomorrow, with another term added for breaking out. And——"

They heard, through the dripping rain, the engine of a car on the hill.

"Listen," said the boy tautly. "I don't want to shoot you. I don't want to shoot anybody. But, so help me God, I will if you try to turn me over! Get up now!" He advanced, holding the revolver in a hand which did not tremble from fear or excitement, nor was there any fear apparent in the old man's face as the gun was pressed against his coat.

"You needn't worry," he said. "I'm not a fool."

Outside, headlights illuminated watery trees. The boy stood, concealed by a curtain, the gun in his hand, as the other opened the door and the uniformed figure of a state trooper dripped in the doorway.

"I won't come in, sir—I'm too wet. The chief sends his

compliments and asks to be excused from the chess game this evening. There's a convict escaped."

"He has a wet night for it," commented the old man.

"Him and us both. Well, good night, Warden."

"Good night, Peters." The door closed; a circle of light swirled as the car turned back up the hill. "I wasn't warden for thirty years without learning something about men," the old man said. "You'd better get going, hadn't you? I'll drop in and see you when you come back."

The boy stared at him, his eyes still suspicious, puzzled; and the old man's eyes dropped to the revolver.

"You don't know much about guns, do you?" He smiled. "That's what we call a Russian model—thirty-two-forty-four —single-action breakdown. Haven't had a bullet for it in twenty years. If you'll just put it back in the drawer as you go out—it was a present, and I'm an old man and sentimental."

THE LION ROARED

Virginia Eiseman

IF a Mr. P. Alfred Merivale ever passes your way, you'd better let me know—Mike Brock, care of The Taproom, Mark Twain Hotel, South Plains, Missouri. If you meet P. Alfred, it's a cinch you'll take a good look at him. He's a big, substantial, white-haired guy like the kind that's always sitting around sipping mint juleps in the whiskey ads.

It was a couple of months ago that he checked in at the Mark Twain. I was behind the bar cutting up fruit, getting set for Cy Archer and Ben Wood and the rest of the gang that drop in around four thirty for old-fashioneds. All of a sudden Timmy the bellboy rushes in, waving a green bill and yelling:

"Say, Mike, this is one for the books! A big shot from Chicago just pulled in, and guess what he asks for. A *suite!* Get a load of that—a *suite!*"

Timmy's laughing, and I get a kick out of it, too. The M. T.'s a mighty fine hotel, but it just doesn't go in for suites or the fancier things in life.

"This dude must have us mixed up with the Waldorf-Astoria," says Timmy. "But you ought to see his bags— three of the smoothest-looking suitcases I've ever had my hands on. And he gave me this buck just for dumping them in his room." Timmy sticks the dollar into a pocket and gets off the stool. He says, "Anyhow, Mike, you'll get a look at this Chicago fellow on account of he's staying two weeks." And then our bellboy breezes out of the bar.

Well, I don't pay much attention to Timmy's story at first, because he gets hysterical when anyone gives him more than a two-bit tip, which isn't often. But I begin wondering why a stranger would make a point of sticking around South Plains for two weeks. Don't get me wrong. This is a great little town, if you're born and raised here. Still, compared to Chicago, it's strictly a dyed-in-the-wool whistle stop.

While I'm sabotaging the chamber of commerce, the lobby door opens and in walks the biggest and most solid-looking citizen I've ever seen. I size him up from top to bottom— from a dark hat like the sort Anthony Eden wears in the newsreels, to spats. The big guy sits himself at the bar and flashes me a smile.

"I'll take the best whiskey you have," he says. "Straight."

As I'm pouring his drink, I say in my most hospitable manner, "You must be the gentleman from Chicago. They tell me you're going to be here for quite a spell."

"For two weeks," he nods. "I'm here for a rest. Doctor's orders." And then he slips off his coat and puts it on the stool beside him.

The minute he straightens up again, I notice something shiny on his suit lapel and I see it's a pin—a gold lion pin. At first I think it's one of those gadgets that college fraternities hand out, but it's too big for that, and I'm about to ask him just what it is. Then I remember I'm the guy who pops olives into martinis, and if the customers go in for screwy jewelry—well, that's none of my business. In the meantime the man from Chicago's keeping up a steady stream of chatter. But the late afternoon mob wanders in, and I have to concentrate so hard on juggling glasses and bottles that I put an end to all conversation.

I'm in the midst of shoving a round of old-fashioneds at Cy Archer, Ben Wood, and Luke Williams when I see that my new pal has moved over a few stools and joined them.

"I'd like to introduce myself," he's saying. "I'm P. Alfred Merivale from Chicago."

A great session of handshaking and backslapping follows, and in half an hour they're making jokes a mile a minute, and Mr. Merivale's fat pigskin wallet does the honors on the next round of drinks. Then all of a sudden Cy Archer, our local banker, snatches some words right out of my mouth.

"Tell us about that lion pin you're wearing," he says. "I've never seen anything like it before, Merivale. Where did it come from?"

"Well, it's a funny thing about this pin," answers Mr. Merivale. "Strange as it may seem, I don't really know where it did come from. I was down in Lima about fifteen summers ago and one afternoon I wandered into a little shop and bought a lot of trinkets. When I got back to my room and unwrapped the package, this gold pin was on top. I took it back to the old Peruvian who'd sold the other stuff to me, and he said he'd never laid eyes on the lion before. So the only thing for me to do was to keep it."

"Why do you wear it?" Luke Williams asks. "Any special reason?"

The big man turns on his smile full blast. "That's another funny story. I suppose I started wearing it because I was impressed with the strange way it appeared out of nowhere. But it turned out to be the luckiest little pin anybody ever wore. I—er—well——" Mr. Merivale acted like he didn't quite know how to say what was coming up. "Well, gentlemen, I realize this is something one doesn't usually discuss, but I've been extremely successful. The reason I mention it is because of the pin. From the second I first saw the lion, the breaks have come my way in everything—oil wells, mines, the stock market, just everything. And it's all due to this little pin here."

"You wouldn't care to swap lions in midstream, would you, Merivale?" asks Cy Archer. "My granddaughter has a stuffed one and I bet I could get her to trade with you. We could use some luck for a change."

Mr. Merivale switches his smile to a laugh. "I'm a superstitious cuss and I wouldn't part with it for anything in the world." Then he notices me. I guess I'm practically leaning into his glass. "Give us another round, will you, Mike?" he says.

Well, during the next week he and his gold lion spend a lot of time with me in the taproom. He does his wining here and his dining with the Archers, the Williamses, and the other South Plains socialites. The number of friends he collects makes Dale Carnegie look like an amateur, and it's all on account of the pin.

ONE morning as I'm hauling cartons of pretzels to the back of the bar, Timmy collides with me. "Did you hear the news about Mr. Merivale?" he pants. "He's lost his lion pin."

Right then and there you could have taken one of those pretzels and knocked me over with it. It seems that the last Mr. Merivale remembers seeing his pin is at the church social the night before, and now he's offering a thousand-dollar reward to anyone who finds it. He's buying a full-page ad in the weekly paper, Timmy tells me.

I feel mighty sorry for Mr. Merivale, who strikes me as being the most high-class barfly I've ever met up with. Then I think long and hard about the thousand bucks which wouldn't do the family kitty of one Mike Brock any harm at all.

Finally, I can't help wondering if the pin is lost, strayed, or stolen. Cy Archer's crack about wanting it comes back to me along with a bunch of others that I've heard.

Mr. Merivale shows up the same as usual later in the day. "Maybe I'm carrying this thing too far," he says to the gang. "You fellows must think I'm crazy to promise such a big reward, because the lion's certainly worth no more than a dollar or two. Still, it's the sentimental value that counts. I've got to go back to Chicago at the end of the week, and I'm hoping the pin will go with me."

"Don't worry, Alf, we'll find it for you," pipes up Cy Archer.

But we don't find it. Mr. Merivale's loss is the town topic all right. People meander about with their eyes glued to the ground, and yet nothing happens—nothing, that is, except the day of P. Alfred's departure rolls around. Right after Timmy brings down his bags, the big man himself comes into the bar.

"I just had to drop in for a quick one," he says. "I couldn't leave South Plains without telling you goodbye, Mike."

I make it clear how sorry I am to see him go, and then we get on the subject of his lion pin.

"That thousand-dollar reward still holds," he tells me. "If you ever hit upon a clue, Mike, you can reach me at the Brownstone in Chicago."

Well, the town seems pretty dreary without Mr. Merivale. Now and then somebody mentions the gold pin, but it still doesn't show up. The crew that's good for a daily old-fashioned or two act like there's been a death in the family—

they're that fond of P. Alfred. They all keep saying how they wish he'd come back.

One afternoon Cy Archer hasn't dropped in yet, but the rest of his cronies are already in a huddle at the bar. Ben Wood has the inspiration that maybe Merivale would like to join them on the fishing trip they're cooking up. Everybody seconds the motion. I don't wait to find out if they're going to phone P. Alfred long-distance because I notice a weird character standing at the end of the bar. He's obviously a member of the school that doesn't believe in haircuts or shaves. I say to myself that I'm now laying eyes on the original washed-up wreck.

"You'd better move along, bud," I tell him in a polite way.

"Give me a shot of whiskey," he says.

I'm about to recommend Harry's Tavern on the other side of town when my eyes almost pop out of my head. There, sitting on top of a patch in this bum's jacket, is Mr. Merivale's gold lion. As fast as I can get the words out, I ask the tramp where he got it.

"Found it by the railroad tracks," is his answer.

I guess I'm making a lot of noise, so some people wander over to see what's up. In the beginning they think they ought to make a mass beeline to the oculist, but Ben Wood is finally willing to believe what he sees. When he asks the guy how much he wants for the pin, they all get busy, and there follows the liveliest auction that's ever taken place in South Plains.

The tramp admits the lion doesn't mean a thing to him. Still, he says, it must mean something to somebody or there wouldn't be all this fuss, and he tells the boys he won't sell it for a cent under five hundred dollars in cash. With a checkbook in one hand and a pen in the other, Luke Williams dashes into the lobby and he's back in a minute with a wad of bills. They go straight into the bum's grimy fist and in exchange Luke gets the gold pin. Nobody gives a hoot when the tramp slips out now; they've lost interest in him.

I'm all for calling Mr. Merivale right away, but Luke wants to buy everyone in the bar a drink first.

"I'm still about four hundred and ninety dollars ahead!" he shouts. "And think how happy this is going to make Alf!"

As I'm knocking myself out setting them up, I see Cy Archer come in with a grin on his face. Luke gives him the high sign, can't wait to tell him the news, but Cy has some words of his own to get in edgewise.

"You'll never believe it, boys," he wheezes. "It's a miracle —an absolute miracle! I just met some broken-down bum outside, and you'll never guess what I bought from him!"

We hicks may not be quiz kids, but that was a five-hundred-dollar question that didn't stump any of us. And if Mr. P. Alfred Merivale is as smart as I know he is, he won't ever again pick South Plains for a rest cure or come sauntering into the Mark Twain looking for a suite.

INITIATION

Burton Rascoe

SCOTTY always has to clean out the bowl of his pipe with a jackknife before he can make a decision or even answer a plain yes or no. If he gouges around in the bowl a long time, it means he has dug around in his memory and dredged up something that always begins, "Did I ever tell you about the time——"

He did it when we were out at Charlie Hawk's cabin in the Kiamichi Mountains. We had just put away the dinner dishes and Charlie had got out the cards for our nightly session of penny-ante poker.

Charlie and I drew up our chairs to the table and waited. Scotty closed his jackknife, filled his pipe, lighted it, and started aimlessly shuffling the cards. He said:

"It was about the time when we was down in San Antone. You got to remember that all through the fracas our cavalry troop had a different sort of status from any other outfit in the service. We had all signed up with the understanding that we wasn't going to have none of that West Point folderol and not a lot of unnecessary drilling to harden us up. We was plenty tough as it was. I don't mean we was mean or bad. We didn't mind getting likkered up now and then and raising a little Cain. But we wasn't mean. We was just hardened up from working and living out in the open. Ranchers, cowhands, blacksmiths, peace officers, and so on.

"Well, they kept us down there in barracks a long time and give us some horses to ride and get acquainted with, except there was one mustang in the bunch that was pretty danged hard to get acquainted with. I never seen a meaner horse in my life. He threw the best bronc buster in the outfit so hard and so fast he crippled that cowhand up something terrible.

"Well, we was getting pretty restless, just sitting around waiting for orders. We didn't have anything to do except gripe about something. And I'm telling you we griped plenty. First we gripes about what we hears we ain't going to elect no boss of our outfit from out amongst ourselves like we thought we would but was going to be bossed by some bird that was coming down from New York. To make matters worse, the rumor got around that this bird was a danged flatfoot. We was plenty sore.

"Well, then one day a lot of crates of rifles arrived and we was told to line up and get them rationed out to us. A West Point shavetail and a coupla regular army top sergeants was temporarily running things.

"Jake Amorine, from Perry, Oklahoma, was standing there alongside when the first case was opened. Jake was as strong as an ox and he knew guns. He picked one of them rifles up and he could tell by the looks and feel of it that it was no damned good. They was those old Krags. They was a tree right behind Jake and he turned around, and danged if he didn't wham the rifle against that tree and wrap the barrel around it.

"They put him under arrest right away, of course. Serious offense, destroying United States property.

"Well, they was leading Jake off to the guardhouse, when Bill Alexander yelled, 'Wait a minute, I'm coming with you!' And darned if Bill didn't grab him one of them guns and wham it against the tree.

"They was leading Jake and Bill away, when a short stocky man with the queerest-looking duds on you ever saw, and wearing goggles—we called specs goggles—came up out of nowhere and shoved his way through the crowd. He yelled, 'Release those men! Come here!' Not until then did we look to notice that he rated a salute.

"Well, they came up and this little cock sparrow asked Jake what was the explanation of his conduct. Jake looked him straight in the eye, mad like, and says, 'I ain't going to fight no war with no damned firecrackers, not for you nor nobody else, mister.'

"I nearly fell over when I heard Jake say that. But danged if that little cock sparrow didn't put out his hand and shake Jake's hand and then Bill's. Then he said, 'You're the kind of men I want in this outfit, men who know guns and have guts enough to say so. You're released. Charges dismissed. At ease.'

"Not until then did it dawn on us that this was the new boss of the outfit, the guy that was supposed to be a New York flatfoot. He told the shavetail to have then Krags shipped back where they came from.

"Then he said he would like to take a look at the horses. We followed him over to the corral. He stood there looking at them for a few minutes and then asked one of the boys if they wouldn't fetch him a bridle and saddle. When they came he took the bridle, and I'm a son of a gun if he didn't make right for that mean mustang I was telling you about.

"This bird went up to the mustang and bridled him. Then he did something that made us know right now that he was no flatfoot. He untied the bandanna handkerchief around his neck and blindfolded the horse. Any good cowboy knows if you blindfold a wild horse or a mean horse so he can't see anything whilst you saddle and mount him, he will stand still.

"Well, Four-eyes blindfolds the horse and then somebody runs out there with the saddle and blanket and saddles him. Four-eyes mounts him and leans over and snatches the handkerchief away.

"Well, I'm telling you I've seen some bucking in my time and some riding, too; but I never seen no meaner bucking and no better riding than that. Four-eyes not only stuck on; he rode that mustang out of the buck and gave him the gaff and rode hell out of him. When it was plain the horse had had enough, Four-eyes threw the reins over the mustang's head and dismounted and the horse just stood there. We knew already that that guy was no New York flatfoot; he knew horses and, what's more, we was ready to follow him through hell and high water from then on. Jake and Bill wanted to go up to him to apologize, and they asked me to go along as spokesman.

"We all saluted and I hemmed and hawed and said we all wanted to apologize. The new boss acted like he didn't know what we was apologizing for; and that made us pretty embarrassed because we didn't know either. Then I said, 'Sir, we didn't exactly maybe get your name just right. Are you Colonel Rosenfeld?'

"He smiled and showed a lot of big white teeth and said,

'You can call me that if you like. The name is Roosevelt. But I imagine you all will soon be calling me Teddy, at least behind my back. I hope so.' "

THE JACKKNIFE

T. F. Healey

IT was a big day for our village when Rory O'More came home from the sea. He had gone on a spree and ended up in the navy, the neighbors said, in the First World War, and had never returned until the fates drove him homewards again after the Second World War.

In all that time there was never a word from him, so that most came to think he was drowned in some green hell of the wide ocean, while a few held that Rory was not a man to die before his time and that he was alive and seeking his fortune in the rich, far places of the earth, maybe having found it to forget entirely the sweet, fair land of his birth.

So when one fine day he was seen limping up the street, there was a great to-do. Housewives ran to their half-doors, old men gasped, dogs barked, and donkeys brayed. Never was such a pother in the village before.

Only, Rory had no fortune, coming back as he had gone, and that was penniless. For all his years away, he had nothing to show for it save the clothes on his back; and it was lucky, they said, that he found a sister still living to take him in. But nobody minded that, for thinking how rich he was in the wealth of the grand adventures he had had and in the great stories about them tumbling around in his mind. And wasn't a good story in Ireland more gold than gold any day?

The fact was that Rory had the village in thrall. Well he knew it, too; he strutted around like a turkey cock, and everywhere he went they put a welcome before him. The big trouble was that it wasn't so easy to get a story out of him, for he had so much to tell that he never knew quite where to begin. Besides, he was a bit touched in the head, they said; and there was a big dent in his skull where he had been hit with a marlinspike during a mutiny in the Indian Ocean.

So they thought the best thing to do was to bring him to call on Malachi Michael O'Hanrahan, the village oldster, who, with the wise Gaelic in him, had much of the lore of the race and was ninety-odd years, and who had known Rory well when he was a young gossoon. And they poured out the golden Irish whiskey, the better to draw one of Rory's stories out of him.

"Och, Rory, my lad, a hundred thousand welcomes to you, and we thinking you cold in the deep, and nobody to give you a wake but the mermaids," said Malachi Michael.

"Well, my time wasn't come," said Rory simply.

"And 'tis the power of the grand stories you must have surely," went on Malachi Michael, "and yourself having followed the wind and wave and the wandering flame over the seven seas and over the hills and the droums and grassy billows of many lands, the way great Homer himself wouldn't be in it with you."

It was a fine compliment from Malachi Michael, everyone in the house thought, to put Rory in the right mood. But Rory sniffed in scorn.

"Stories! Stories, is it?" he said. "Sure, I've stories on top of stories, but where'd I begin? Oh, boys, oh, boys, the sights I've seen would make you all go daft to be hearing them, till you'd be hounding me and pestering me till the end of my days for more, you would. Sure, sure, I've seen everything."

The house was hushed now, waiting to hear a tale out of the glorious Iliad of his wanderings.

"Sure, I've seen them all," he went on, "the countries and the provinces and the isles and the islets, the peninsulies and the archipeligies, from the Rhine to the Amyzone, from Cayro to Calcutty and from Frisco to Ishtanboole. Oh, boys, oh, boys, is it the Tadgy McHale you want me to tell you about, and it set on a lake of silver and gold, and the marble courts with the white fountains, or the stairways you'd be climbing to see the little brown gods of the East? Boys, oh, boys, when I think of the lands of gold——"

Malachi Michael cut him short, to the disappointment of everyone. "Gold, is it?" he said. "And why didn't you bring some of it back with you?"

Rory drank, pursed his lips, and looked in disdain at the rafters.

"I had scads of gold, only, what with the drink and the devil, I spent it, and it went through my hands like water under the mill. Sure didn't I have gifts and tokens and spoils of gold galore, but what did I care! I lost everything I had, and when did an O'More ever give a damn about anything like that! But where was I now? In Madras or in Samarkand? You'd be hounding me till the end of my days to be telling you the——"

" 'Tis the wild devil you always were," broke in Malachi Michael, "and you riding life withershins and in the high boot."

"There was the time when," continued Rory, ignoring him "—but where was I now, in Algiers or in Singypoore? No, be damned to it, 'twas in Rangoon where—pass me that bottle till I tell you."

THE house jumped the seas with him and waited quietly until he filled his tumbler. But Malachi Michael broke the spell again by bringing his thoughts back home.

"Isn't it the good thing, Rory, to be back in the sod of your birth and to feel the turf strength under your feet?"

Rory fidgeted. "Ah, well," he said, "sure I came home only at the heel of the hunt and to die in the end maybe as soft as any old cow in a boghole, and all you'll be saying after me is asking if you'll get your bellyful of the whiskey at my wake. But 'tis go away again I would now, save for the rheumatiz in my bones. But where was I now when——"

" 'Twas in Rangoon, Rangoon!" the house shouted as one.

"Rangoon, was it? Let me have that bottle, and sure I feel like perishing it all. Rangoon was a place I'll be long forgetting, for 'twas where I got the diamond to make me rich as a maharajy himself, only a woman crossed my path and finagled it out of me, bad cess to her."

"Och, 'twas the greenhorn you were surely," said Malachi Michael. "Did you lose your senses along with everything else?"

"Tell us the story about the woman and the diamond, Rory," went up a plea from the house.

"The back of my hand to her," said Rory. "May she marry a ghost and bear him a kitten, and may the High King of Glory give her the gout. She fooled me, she did, and by the holy brow of Buddha, she——"

And now a great murmur of disapproval went up as Malachi Michael broke in again, pointing the shank of his clay pipe at Rory.

"Is it Buddha you swear by now?" he thundered. "And is it a pagan you are and not Irish at all, saving your brogue, God bless it! Och, to speak in fewness and truth, 'tis more than your fortune you lost, Rory O'More."

Rory paused and pursed a scornful underlip. "My respects to you, Malachi Michael," he said, "but what would yourself be knowing about it that never went anywhere out of the barony? And is it crying after this little patch of a place you'd have me be, and myself going over the great foreign world this thirty years and more?"

"The winds of the world don't always blow wisdom into a man's head," said Malachi Michael, "and maybe the wisest men are those who stay home. But 'tis a long time surely you've been gone. I don't suppose now you'd be remembering the day you left, would you?"

" 'Tis a long ways back you go, taxing my memory," replied Rory in a great silence of disappointment, for by this time the house had given up all hope of a story. "But where was I now when you interrupted me, in Oiran or in Zanzybare? No, 'twas in Timbuktu, was it?"

"WOULD you be remembering the present we gave you, and you leaving?" asked Malachi Michael.

"Present? Present? Pass me that bottle," said Rory.

"Och, sure the fine jackknife we gave you the day you left us, for winning that hurling game against Ardhoona and upholding the honor of our little village."

"A game, was it?" mumbled Rory.

"You played hell-for-leather that day, Rory, like a hero of old, and drove in the winning goal, and all for our little village. But I suppose you've long forgot all about it."

Rory paused and swallowed his tumbler of whiskey. He looked over at Malachi Michael; an old memory filled his sea-sad eyes, and the music of a wistful smile played over his weathered face.

"For the little village I was born in," he said softly, as if to himself. "It reminds me now, and 'twas well you mentioned it, Malachi Michael, for that I kept and still have here in the same place all the days of my willful life. I lost everything else, but sure I never lost that, and here it is now."

Rory fumbled a bit, fished in his jacket, and pulled the jackknife from a pocket.

"By the scepter of Patrick," laughed Malachi Michael, "if that isn't the great story itself and better than all your foreign ones, Rory!"

"Well, now," muttered Rory, "—well—well, maybe."

"And let us bring out more of the whiskey and the glad

tobacco. We'll wet that story and drink to it this night for a merrimented time."

And there was a great hush on the house.

SCARECROW

Paul Jones

EDDIE GANN was hiding out after the Unionville Bank job when he came along the rutted yellow road by Herkimer's farm and bargained a week's food and lodging against the repair of a rusty tractor. That evening he walked ten miles to get off a telegram to Nosey Flynn, so that Nosey would know where to send him some money and the address where the gang would meet again.

He expected an answer in three days; but the R.F.D. carrier passed on the third morning without a sign. Meanwhile he had learned that Herkimer was deputy tax collector for the district, and, following a new idea, he killed Herkimer with a heavy wrench as the farmer stooped over a water pail.

When Eddie opened Herkimer's wallet, he found ninety-one dollars and a statement of tax receipts showing that sum as the total collected. Eddie almost laughed. He expected two Gs from Nosey Flynn. This wouldn't do him any good.

He'd still have to wait for the letter. That meant the body had to be hidden. But where? Gann thought desperately of a dozen places, his small, mean eyes darting over house and barn. The well? Too obvious. Under the hay in the loft? Anybody would think of that at once. The body ought to be buried, but the ground was dry with drought and any fresh digging would show immediately. Except in the cornfield! That was it. Herkimer had cultivated the rows only the day before; the earth was freshly turned. It would be easy to make a shallow grave.

There was only a little blood, and that was matted into Herkimer's thick blond hair. Gann hoisted the body over one shoulder and carried it through the farmyard into the green sea of corn. The place to bury it, he thought, was well beyond the scarecrow, up by the wood lot.

The soft earth made hard walking with a heavy weight, and when he came to the scarecrow, Gann let the body down while he caught his breath in gasps. At that moment he heard a car humming at the valley grade and was panic-stricken. But his terror inspired him. After a moment's hesitation, he ripped the scarecrow from its stout upright and crosspiece, and pulled the ragged coat over Herkimer's torso. Then he set the corpse up on its feet, braced the stiffening arms over the crosspiece and jammed the felt hat over its face.

When the strange car pulled up at the farm gate, Eddie was getting a drink at the well curb. A tall, loose-jointed man got out of the new black sedan and walked over.

"Herkimer around?" he asked.

"He's away on a trip."

"When'll he be back?"

"He didn't say." Under the other's cool gaze, Eddie offered further explanation: "I'm just here working on his tractor."

"Funny. He's supposed to have some tax money for me. Guess I'll wait for him. I'm the road commissioner."

"Suit yourself."

Eddie went back of the barn and pretended to work while the afternoon wore away. The scarecrow was not a hundred yards from where he stood, and the more he looked at it the more his confidence grew. Nobody could tell the difference. He could stay until morning, make sure of his letter, and make a clean getaway.

At sundown, going through the barn to the house, he saw that the stranger had run his sedan under cover to protect the finish, and a brilliant idea struck him. The black sedan was just what he needed for a fast break in the morning. He detached a wire from the ignition and put it in his pocket.

For dinner Eddie and the commissioner ate bacon and bread and drank black coffee. "I can't figure where Herkimer got to," the stranger complained.

"Maybe he skipped with the tax money."

"I don't think so."

"I was only kidding," Eddie said hastily.

When the commissioner gave up hope of seeing Herkimer and went to his car, he was unable to start it. "Stay all night," Eddie urged. "Herkimer'll turn up, and I'll fix your car for you when I can see what I'm doing."

"Guess there's nothing else I can do. I'm fifty miles from home."

"Sure; stick around."

Back in the house, Eddie thought of another angle. This guy was collecting taxes. He might have a lot of jack on him. Might be a nice bit of business to knock him off while he was asleep. But he abandoned that notion when he saw that the stranger had an automatic on the table by his bed.

It was funny, what little things gave him the jumps. For just a minute Eddie wondered if the guy did think something was screwy about Herkimer's being away. But why shouldn't a collector of taxes carry a rod? He'd be a sap if he didn't.

In the morning Eddie awoke with a secret assurance that he identified as a lucky hunch. Today's the day, he thought. Today the letter comes. He felt hot. Nothing could go wrong now.

When the R.F.D. carrier pulled up at the gate, Eddie and the commissioner were standing there waiting for him. The commissioner had his face turned toward the cloudless blue of the sky.

"Here's your letter." The carrier handed an envelope to Eddie. "Herkimer around?"

"He went away on a trip."

The mailman got out of the car to stretch his legs. "Over to see his sister, I reckon. Heard she was poorly. What you looking at, Commissioner?"

The feel of the letter told Eddie it had money in it.

The other two were staring upward. Just like a couple of corn-feds, Eddie thought. Always trying to guess the weather, like a ticket speculator on the day of a big game.

"That makes twelve of them," the commissioner remarked.

"Thirteen, I make it—and there's two more!"

They continued to stare. Eddie looked up carelessly—and stiffened with fear. A flock of wheeling birds went round and round over the scarecrow. And as he watched, the boldest of the buzzards lunged downward in a lazy swoop, and knocked the hat from Herkimer's white and rigid face.

THE PERFECT MURDER

Roy L. Mangum

FOR twenty-two years Mark Melcher had walked from his drugstore to his house at exactly five o'clock. Methodical, Mark was. For twenty-two years he had been greeted respectfully along the way by men and women who had grown old with him. Dignified, Mark was. For twenty-two years he had stopped to pat the heads of children, and give them penny candies. Kindly, Mark was. "Wouldn't hurt a fly," as Bob Barstow, the sheriff, often said.

Mark was Willowville's best-loved citizen, all right. People came to him with their troubles. Behind his old, dusty prescription counter he listened to the secrets of human beings who trusted him. He had a way about him, Mark had, so that you listened to his advice, and carried it out, and found yourself the better for it.

Emily Holden was a mighty pretty girl of about twenty-two. The schoolteacher, and a good one. Even the pupils liked her. She had come to Willowville early in September and by Christmas she was dead in love with Andrew Fellows. Old Man Fellows—he wasn't so very old, though, come to think of it—was the richest man in town and head of the school board. So, naturally, he saw a lot of Emily Holden. She went up to his house now and then to talk over school matters, and it was plain to see, after a spell, that she was gone over him. Not just in love, you understand, but crazy about him—like some women get over a man.

Well, Emily came into Mark Melcher's drugstore one day and got behind the prescription counter and began to take on something awful. Mark listened to her story, and while she was telling it his eyes got to looking mighty ugly.

"And you say Andrew Fellows is the man?" he demanded when she got through.

"Oh, I have been such a fool!" Emily sobbed. "But I loved him so, and he promised to marry me. And now he threatens to tell something he says he knows about me, Mr. Melcher. Something he says is terrible. Oh, what shall I do, Mr. Melcher?"

Mark put his arms around Emily Holden and held her close and cried. It was awful. Pretty soon he pulled himself together and went to the bank and cashed a fat check. Then he came back and gave Emily the money.

"You go," he said, "to this address"—he gave her the name of somebody in New York—"and tell the lady there all about it. Tell her Mark Melcher sent you. And don't you ever come back to Willowville, Emily."

Emily insisted she couldn't take the money, of course. But Mark just took her in his arms and kissed her mighty tenderly and made her do it. Then, when she had gone, he got behind his prescription counter again and waited.

He had made up his mind to kill Old Man Fellows, to confess, and to let them hang him if they wanted to.

Pretty soon Old Man Fellows came in to ask for some of the eyewash he usually bought.

"Got a new kind, Andrew," Mark said slowly. "Smells nice, too."

He went behind the counter and got a half ounce of prussic acid. The pure stuff, undiluted. Then he let Old Man Fellows take a little whiff of it.

"Smells sort of like peach blossoms," said Old Man Fellows. "Kind of nice, isn't it?"

"It's nice," said Mark, "and just as good for the eyes as it smells. I've only got this much, but I'll let you have it, same price as the other."

Old Man Fellows smiled. Mark did too, for he knew that a single drop of pure prussic acid inside the eye would kill Old Man Fellows almost as quick as lightning.

Old Man Fellows paid over his money and started to leave. It was five o'clock, so Mark went along with him. At his house Mark turned in and bade his friend goodbye.

Early next morning the news spread like wildfire. Mrs. Thompson, Old Man Fellows' housekeeper, had found him deader than a doornail when she went upstairs to see what had kept him so long before breakfast. Near her master in the bathroom she had found a little bottle, and gripped in Old Man Fellows' hand, so tightly that he had crushed it, was an eyedropper.

AT FIVE o'clock that afternoon Mark Melcher closed his store, locked it, and walked over to the sheriff's office. He was going to confess, and clear his conscience, and make his peace with God, even if they hanged him for it. He didn't care now what happened.

"Bob," he said to the sheriff, "I've come to give myself up. I killed Andrew Fellows."

The sheriff started to laugh, but one look at Mark's eyes stopped him. Wild-looking and sort of glassy they were—like crazy people's eyes. The sheriff told Mark to sit down and went outside for a minute to whisper something to his deputy.

"Mark Melcher's goin' crazy," he said. "He thinks he killed Old Man Fellows. Can you beat it? Why, Mark wouldn't hurt a fly. Too bad. They was friends for years, those two. Guess it must have hit Mark pretty hard."

That news spread like wildfire, too. Mark Melcher had gone kind of crazy over Old Man Fellows' death! Wasn't it a shame? And Mark such a fine man. So sympathetic. Too sympathetic, he was, worrying himself crazy over his friend's death because he had sold him some poison. As if he could have known that Old Man Fellows was going to commit suicide, like the coroner said!

He got to wandering around Willowville, telling everybody he had killed Old Man Fellows. Folks would listen, shake their heads, and say, "That's too bad, Mark. That's too bad." Then they'd walk on. Pretty soon Mark got so he would wake up at night and scream. His housekeeper left him.

They put Mark away in Doc Smith's sanitarium. Everybody says it's too bad, and they can't imagine how Mark Melcher ever got the idea that he killed Old Man Fellows.

But then, Willowville folks don't know to this day that Emily Holden was Mark Melcher's daughter, that Mark had never been married, and that Old Man Fellows was the only human being on earth who knew those things.

THE MAN FROM LIBERTY STREET

Paul MacNamara

This story first turned up in Stockholm, back in early 1940. No one knows where it started or who told it first.

At least there is one thing all versions agree on, and that's the date. It was the day after Henderson, the British Ambassador to Germany, left Berchtesgaden for London for the last time.

That would be the end of August, 1939. The whole business took place in less than twenty minutes at Hitler's aerie, "Eagle's Nest," on that fateful day.

Eagle's Nest, as you probably know, is a fantastic place perched on the top of Kehlstein, a queer towerlike rock formation eighteen hundred feet high in the Bavarian mountains not far from Berchtesgaden, Hitler's country home. The main room was huge, glass-enclosed on three sides, giving a tremendous airplane view of the surrounding mountains. It was probably designed for the Nazi party's and Adolf Hitler's personal shrine. On Hitler's desk in the great room used to lie the famous Wotan's Hand.

The story goes that one day, when the place was being built, Hitler stumbled on the curious piece of rock shaped exactly like a giant human hand. It fascinated him and he had it mounted in a glass case and explained to visitors that it was the hand of the German god of war. He was known to be greatly attached to it and believed it to be the symbol of good luck.

One thing more, important to the story, is that all who saw Eagle's Nest in its palmier days agreed it was unquestionably one of the most inaccessible houses in the world and certainly one of the most closely guarded.

So much for background.

The story:

Late in the afternoon of the fateful day, there were gathered together in the glass-enclosed room the top members of the Nazi party and the German General Staff. It was the final meeting before the invasion of Poland and the beginning of World War II.

Twenty-odd men were present, including Göring, Hess, Göbbels, Himmler, and Von Ribbentrop.

The men were gathered in front of a gigantic mounted map of Europe. Hitler was sitting on the edge of his desk, one hand resting on the glass case enclosing the famous Wotan's Hand.

Herr Von Britch, foremost meteorologist in the world, was reading his report and prophecy on the weather for the coming weeks in Europe. The report was good. It would be dry, the panzers would roll easily.

Suddenly—and to this day no one knows how he could have gained admission into that impregnable mountain retreat —a man appeared at Hitler's side.

He was tall and thin and his hair was snow-white. He wore nose glasses attached to a wide black ribbon. In his buttonhole he wore a white carnation.

"Are you Hitler?"

His sudden appearance stunned the room, but when he spoke, it roared into action. Officers lunged toward him. Himmler screamed, "Mueller, damn you!" (Mueller was captain of the SS Guards in charge of guarding Hitler.) The room was in a panic. Somewhere a siren began to whine.

Hitler held up his hand. "Wait."

The stranger was smiling. He seemed unconcerned at the commotion he had caused. He had taken off his glasses and was polishing them with his handkerchief. "Sorry if I interrupted, but I heard that you gentlemen were interested in acquiring some real estate and I thought I might help."

Himmler had drawn his Luger and was pointing it at the

man's heart. "How did you get in here, and who are you?"

Hitler pushed the pistol to one side. "Acquire real estate—what do you mean?"

The stranger began to polish his glasses again.

"I have heard the complaint many, many times in Germany—that forty-six million Englishmen rule forty million kilometers, while eighty-five million Germans rule only half a million square kilometers. I have heard you make this complaint yourself, Herr Hitler."

The stranger continued, "It was my understanding that this meeting today has to do with this discrepancy. Isn't that right?"

As the man talked, Hitler stood looking at him, with his feet apart, cradling his elbow in one hand and stroking his mustache reflectively. The man seemed to have him under a spell. He nodded slowly. "It is true. We are interested in *Lebensraum* for the German people. But tell me, what is it to you?"

The man was straightening the handkerchief in his breast pocket. "Because I think I can get it for you, and at a lower price than you will otherwise have to pay."

Von Ribbentrop sneered. "Wholesale, no doubt."

The man ignored him.

"Tell me exactly what you want—how many square kilometers, how much oil, how much steel and coal—everything. Then I will tell you what I think the price will be that you will have to pay. If the price you give is lower than I think I can get it for you, why," the man shrugged, "then I'm wrong. Forget the whole thing."

He took a few steps toward a portable blackboard being used by meteorologist Von Britch. "May I use this?" Hitler nodded.

He drew a double white line down the middle. On one side he wrote, "Wanted by Germany," then turned to the room. "If I put it all down in black and white, I think you will see how simple it is."

He began to write. "One million ten-acre farms outside of the present German borders"; then wrote after it, in small letters, "Land must be productive and fertile." He turned to the room. "Would that be enough new farmland to satisfy the question of living space?"

Hitler imperceptibly nodded his head. The rest of the room was silent.

Then he wrote, "Iron and Steel—twice again the amount

now available in your Saar Basin." He turned to the room. "Okay?" The room was silent.

"Hydraulic Power"—the scratch of the chalk was the only sound in the room—"twice the capacity of Niagara Falls." The men stared silently and the list grew.

"Oil," "Aluminum," "Wheat," and so on until there was nothing left he could think of.

"Well, gentlemen, I must say you really have quite an order here. Now, then, the next question is what are you prepared to pay?"

Göring spoke for the first time. "Pay, you fool! Who said anything about paying? We are taking only what rightfully belongs to us, the master race! *Heil* Hitler!"

The stranger smiled. "Perhaps you are right, Herr Göring, but the cost of—shall we say—collecting will be something."

The man stepped to the blackboard again and on the other side of the double line he had previously drawn he wrote another head: "Cost—to Germany."

"Now, then, let me list some of the costs if you take it by force of arms." He picked up the chalk.

"It will take at least three, maybe four—possibly five years of war to collect all of this." He pointed to the first line. "Now, then, that will mean five, six, perhaps seven million men—*Germans*, who will have to lay down their lives to accomplish the collection of what you say belongs to you. Let's say six million to be conservative." He wrote it down: "Six million Germans," then in parentheses he added, "(dead)."

Underneath he wrote, "Planes." "How many, Herr Göring, are you prepared to throw into it? Two hundred thousand—three hundred thousand—four hundred thousand war planes? Let's say three hundred thousand." And the list began to grow: Tanks, Guns, Halftracks, Oil, Submarines—on and on until the list of arms and armament filled the board.

"Now, then, let's reduce it all to marks. Take the first item of six million dead Germans—soldiers. There must be some price the families of these men would pay if their men were to be allowed to live. Let's be conservative—say five thousand marks from each family. That would be thirty billion marks right there." He wrote "30 billion" opposite the item "Six million Germans."

Opposite "Planes" he wrote "450 billion," and on down the list—"400 billion, 300 billion, 250 billion, 100 billion" —until opposite each item was its value in marks.

Under the last item he drew a line and added up the list. It came to an unbelievable figure running into quintillions of marks.

He put the chalk in the tray and wiped the dust from his hands and turned to face the room. "That, gentlemen, is what you are prepared to pay at this moment for what you want, and the chances are the price will be higher. For some reason, prices always are higher in a war."

He turned and pointed to the first list he had made. "Commission me to go out and buy these things that you want. I am sure I can get them all for you for this staggering amount of money that you say you are prepared to spend. Besides, I'll have something left over. All you have to do is say go ahead.

"For example, in Poland and the Ukraine there must be many farmers who would be willing to sell their land at the high prices I could pay with the vast amounts of money you are prepared to spend. It will take some time, but no longer than it will to fight a war.

"Land in Africa is cheap and very rich. No doubt I can get many fine farms there at even lower prices."

Hitler was silent and the man continued: "As for coal and iron, I am fairly sure the Czechs would sell a part of their holdings, particularly at the high prices you can apparently afford to pay. The same is true of hydraulic power.

"Remember, it won't be the first time a country has bought great land riches with money. Where I come from we once bought several hundred thousand square miles for seven million dollars—less by far than you will put into fighter planes for one month, Herr Göring. I am speaking of Alaska, of course.

"Well, gentlemen, what do you say? Why not roll up your war maps? Believe me, I can get it for you easier and cheaper. It may take a little time, but, as I said, not so long as a war will take. And besides, with my plan you will get what you want, while with yours the chances are you won't. Oh, yes, and another thing. With my plan I said you will have something left over—I was referring to the six million German soldiers that you won't have if you do it your way." He paused. "Well, Herr Hitler, what do you say?"

Himmler's finger tightened on the trigger of his pistol. For a minute the room was filled with smoke and the vibration of the shot.

"I take it your answer to my suggestion is no. I'm sorry, because I think you will regret it."

The smoke cleared, but the stranger had disappeared. Yet Himmler's pistol couldn't have been more than six feet from him when he had pulled the trigger.

Göbbels limped over to pick up something on the floor where the man had been standing. It was a small white business card. He read it slowly, out loud: "Joseph P. Day, Realtor, 67 Liberty Street, New York City." When he finished, he handed it to Hitler, whose hand was outstretched for it.

Von Ribbentrop repeated the name, "Joseph P. Day. That's exactly who that was. I remember seeing his picture not long ago in *Time* magazine."

As he read, Hitler slumped into a chair, turning the little white card over and over in his hands. Somehow he seemed to have lost interest in what Von Britch was saying. He was looking reflectively out the window. If he had looked at the glass case at his elbow containing Wotan's Hand, he would have been shocked to see that Himmler's shot had cracked the great stone hand directly across the knuckles.

THE SECOND BOTTLE

James Ronald

THAT was a cold hard winter and I'm the boy that knew it. The river was frozen solid; you looked down from the bridges and saw the ore barges, gripped tight by the ice and stuck fast there, waiting for the first spring thaw. That year they had a long wait. The wind went through you like a knife and so did the looks they gave you, the people of the town, when they saw you were a stranger. They didn't have jobs enough for their own and it was a cinch they didn't have a job for you. You can't write home for money when the only home you can remember is an orphanage. When you graduate from one of those places, boy, you're on your own. When I got real hungry, I pawned my overcoat for two bucks. That was asking for pneumonia, a cold hard winter like that, but I was a kid at the time, and when you're a kid and you're hungry you gotta eat, that's all there is to it, you gotta eat.

I went into this diner. It wasn't much, a hole in the wall. And ain't this a laugh: I had two bucks in my pocket, but I was so cold, so hungry, I couldn't get the words out when the Greek asked what I wanted to eat. I just sat there, shaking all over, opening and shutting my mouth and not a word coming out.

The Greek gave me a hard look and I figured he was going to bounce me out on my ear. I tried to tell him, "It's okay, I've got money," but the words wouldn't come. He kept looking at me, and after a while, I saw he wasn't sore anymore.

"Hungry?" he said; and I couldn't even answer that. All I could do was nod.

"I been hungry, too," he said; and, believe it or not, he set me up a hamburger and a cup of java. While I ate he kept looking at me, and soon he said maybe he had a job for me. Did I ever work in a restaurant? he asked. I said I had been a dishwasher for a spell and a busboy for another spell. He said his night counterman had quit on him. Not much of a job, they didn't do much business at night, but at least a guy could eat.

"A buck a night and meals," he said, "and you work from ten until three in the morning. How's about it?"

I didn't kiss him but I sure did feel like it. So then he gave me another hamburger and more java and told me the other side of the picture. The catch was that the night chef was a sonuvagun to work with. He didn't like nobody and he made no bones about it.

"You gotta keep out of his kitchen," said the Greek. "You gotta keep out of his way if you don't want no trouble."

"I don't want no trouble," I said.

"Then don't bother him," said the Greek. "Keep away from him. Shout your orders through the hatch and don't get in his way."

I said, "I won't get in his way," and, believe me, I meant it. Well, it wasn't ten yet, but I went behind the counter and started working, figuring the sooner I learned the ropes, the better. The Greek stuck around until midnight, until he saw I'd got the hang of things, and then he told me good night and went home.

There wasn't nothing to it. Only, you got lonely. Some of the time you'd have two or three guys sitting on the stools, reading papers and smoking cigarettes and drinking java and eating hamburgers or scrambled eggs; and some of the time you'd have one lone cabdriver killing time, waiting for a call; but most of the time you had the place to yourself. Just you behind the counter and the sonuvagun of a night chef out there in his kitchen. And, I'm telling you, it got lonely.

ALONG about two thirty the place was empty, then in came this old man and humped himself up on a stool at the back. He was pretty shabby, but he wasn't a bum. There was a kinda funny look about him, but I couldn't figure out what was wrong. He kept touching his coat, high up, on the left side, as if he had something hidden there and wanted to be sure it was still there.

He said, "Coffee," and I brought it to him. I noticed his hands. They kept shaking, and when he picked up the spoon it tinkled on the side of the cup. And then I got a whiff of his breath and it was enough to knock you down. So I thought to myself, That's what it is, that's why he looks so funny, that's why he's got the shakes; he's plastered, he's cock-eyed.

I walked down to the window to see if it was raining. Ten times in an hour I'd walked over to the window to see if it was raining; it helped to pass the time. This time it *was* raining, and I thought to myself, I'm going to get wet as hell if it don't stop before we close up. When I walked back along the counter, I saw that the old man was all hunched up over his java and he was crying as if his heart would break.

The way I am now, if I see someone crying, I look the other way. I leave them cry. It don't matter who, a little child, an old woman, even my own mother—if I'd know her if I saw her. I leave them cry. But this is before I learned my lesson. I was young, I was soft. I saw this old man crying into his java and it made me feel like crying too. I went over to him to see if maybe I could help.

Do you know what hell looks like? It's black and cold and a long way down with no bottom to it. I know, because I've seen it. I seen it in that old man's eyes. He looked at me like he didn't even see me. There was hell staring out of his eyes, and I felt the flesh crawling all the way up my back.

"She had it coming," he said. "She asked for it. A man's got a right to take a drink once in a while. She'd got no call to nag at me the way she did."

He was staring at me, and I had to say something, but I didn't know what to say. "She'll get over it," I mumbled. "Maybe by the time you go back she'll be over it already."

"She won't never get over it," he said. "This time I fixed her good."

I looked back over my shoulder, to see if someone had opened the door. All of a sudden there was a draft of cold air in the place. But the door was shut.

"She's lying back there, on the floor, with half her head blown off," said the old man. "You could go and holler in her ear, but she wouldn't stir. I know. I tried. I hollered in her ear, but she never moved a muscle."

He looked at me again and I got another glimpse of hell. He was in agony, he was on fire, he was burning up inside. The tears were running down his cheeks, but his eyes were black and cold, like ice. And I knew he wasn't kidding. I could tell this wasn't a pipe dream. She had kept nagging at him, and this time he had fixed her good.

And then I noticed this bulge, like there was something in his breast pocket. He kept touching it to make sure it was still there. All of a sudden I knew what it was. It was a gun. It was the gun he had killed her with.

"I don't want to go back there," he said in a whimpering voice. "She's lying there, on the floor. I don't want to go back. I don't want to look at her."

I took two steps back and that brought me to the kitchen door. I took another step back and I was inside. I heard a sound like a snarl and looked round—and there was the sonuvagun of a chef glaring at me. He looked sore enough to stick me with the long knife he had in his hand.

"Get the hell out of my kitchen," he said; and he meant right now.

"Look," I said. "There's a crazy guy out there. He's got a gun."

"Don't give me no lip," said the chef, scowling and taking a step forward. "Get the hell out."

I went back where I came from, and the old man was still there, crying. He looked at me as if he didn't like me, as if he was sorry for what he'd told me. And I thought to myself, He's got a gun. Maybe he'll fix me so I can't tell anyone else. It was so cold I was shivering, and yet the sweat was bursting out on my face and hands.

And then the door opened and a cop came in. I was never so glad to see anyone in all my life. His uniform was glistening with rain. He didn't look at the old man. He humped